THE ORPHAN OF HENGISTBURY HEAD

Mel Flavell

BOOK 3

THE ORPHAN OF HENGISTURY HEAD – Book 3

Table of Contents

MAP OF STONE CIRCLES TRIBE TO SEA

MAP OF RIVERS STOUR & AVON TO HENGISTBURY

CHARACTERS IN ORDER OF APPEARANCE

Lucca	Hunter from the Five Rivers Tribe. Enemy of Henge.
Henge	Master storyteller of Hengistbury.
Minos	Orphan of Littledown Potters.
Beako	Potter of Littledown.
Otto	His underling.
Fredi	The same.
Tarsus	Chief of the Riversmeet Tribe.
Lord Orris	Chief of the 5 Rivers Tribe.
Lady Raisa	His wife.
Mother Ava	Mother to the tribe.
Horsa	Lord Orris' son.
Halstatt	Chief Tarsus' son.
Dugo	His second son.

PROLOGUE - A DANGEROUS ENEMY LET LOOSE

Scourged and humiliated, Lucca retreated into the forest. The people of the Roundwood Tribe had pronounced sentence and banishment after he had stolen another man's horse. Such a crime was punishable by humiliation and a public whipping witnessed by all those travellers still at the Gathering.

As he tramped further away from the Roundwood Summer Gathering, the soreness of his beating burned, and his sense of humiliation grew. Would he never be safe from this young man, Henge? Only by being rid of him on this earth. He thought.

He knew deep inside, instincts told him, that now that Henge had grown into a man, that he would seek justice for the degradation the younger man had witnessed those many years previously. That winter of bitter famine and grief that had left their tribe starving and full of woe.

When the Hunters of the Five Rivers Tribe had ravaged the Stone Circles Tribe, Keepers of the Celestial wisdom. First their intention had been to steal food to feed their starving tribe. Seeing that the grain stores were full, without having been used to help their starving neighbours, and knowing that the priests' predictions had been false, the hunters had been filled with rage. In their anger, they had abused the women and left them for dead.

"Kill them all." They shouted in their frenzy. The eyes of the children still haunted Lucca's sleep, his depth of depravity flashed in front of his half-awake nightmares.

Henge, had been the one surviving witness to what had been done. Now, years later, he had reached such a magnificent stature of young manhood, Lucca thought that the young man would not rest until he had revenged his mother's death. The hunter instinctively knew that, and had foolishly thought to strike first, by stealing the man's horse, trying to make the younger man fear him. It was too late for that, for now Henge was a fully grown man of some stature who had learnt to deal in this world. The young man was now hardened in mind as well as in body with all his skills, to take on the Hunters. Lucca thought. Now they would get no rest until the matter was settled – to the death.

But would he achieve this, skulking here in the forest? No! The best hope he had of ridding himself of his enemy was to outwit and out-manoeuvre his adversary.

Now that Lucca was out of the fearsome wood, onto the plain, the first rays of the morning sun began to appear, and with it, his return of resolve. He would travel faster and rally his fellow hunters in a bid to take over the tribe, while Lord Orris was still making his way home to their Encampment. With their backing he would show Lord Orris who was master and have the loyalty of the other Hunters to take on Henge. For, did they not all bear the stain of that winter of carnage. And Henge was their only witness.

Lucca dusted himself down and drew his cloak around him. The first feeling of renewed pride entered his soul. Yes. He would outwit Lord Orris and Henge at one stroke and would call upon the Hunters to set a trap for this witness to the deeds of all.

Then, with a last look at the glow over the sea, he set a course North West towards the river again, in a direction that would allow him to cross it and back to their encampment before there would be any sign of the returning party.

CHAPTER ONE - HENGE'S RETURN

Hengistbury Head, the following morning.

Henge lay on his bed of bracken and heather and looked up through his canopy of willow branches at an early morning sun, for it was two days after the summer Solstice and he would remember that morning until his dying day.

When, in his sleep beside the river ford where the horses had been corralled, he had imagined that his dreams had been peopled by a beautiful maiden. A nymph of the river in all her natural beauty. But later, when he had also thought to bathe in that same spot, had been caught unawares as he had heard the thunder of hooves beyond the bramble hedge.

Reaching for his goatskin coat, he had been startled to see a young maiden vaulting on and off his colt. A beautiful young woman, with breath-taking skills, as she cavorted on and off the animal's back. His horse, seeing his master as he galloped towards the hedge, put his two forequarters firmly in the ground, coming swiftly to a halt. This catapulted his passenger into and over the blackberry bush, to land at Henge's naked feet!

Oh, what a moment that had been! Both of them startled by the meeting, but arousing anger in the young woman at his presence, and indignation from him, at her presumption to ride his horse! This had led to a fiery exchange of words. But the torch had been lit and it was love at first sight!

Remembering that moment again, Henge awakened from the most peaceful sleep he had ever experienced and jumped up, his head already fired with tasks to be put into action. Henge had returned to the headland full of hope. He now began to plan an ambitious building to prepare for his prospective bride's coming. Henge could not believe that he had really thought a return to the Five Rivers Tribe was possible, as if nothing had happened. Of course, his own life had moved on, and the same distrust and jealousy existed amongst the Hunters of the tribe. Lucca, one of the hunters that had devasted Henge's own tribe during the winter of hunger, would not allow that. Hadn't Lucca shown his vindictiveness at the Roundwood Gathering by trying to steal his colt.

Well, the man had paid for his avarice by the whipping he had received for the theft, at the hands of the Forest Verderers. A crime in their eyes.

Now Henge knew that he would never go back to live with the Five Rivers Tribe. Indeed, now he had no wish to do so, for there was another focus for his life. The amazing acrobat that had taken the liberty of riding his colt, had accepted the gift of the horse and consented to return with the Entertainers at the Autumn Equinox and to marry him in the spring.

But he did not forget at the back of his thinking, that Lucca was an ever-present malign figure who would have to be confronted sometime. For by being punished by the Elders of the Roundwood Tribe by a scourging of willow branches, this was a humiliation that Lucca would not forgive or forget.

In the meantime, for Henge, July came and went, each day filled with sweat and toil. Keeping his fire alight, alternating with chopping and hefting timber with his mare. He drove green timber stakes into the ground to mark out the limits of his possession of the land which would form roots to enclose this space with hedging.

High above as he worked, larks trilled as they soared into the heavens. Their song keeping him company all the while. He went to bed exhausted by his labours, but with spirit renewed by the thought of his new love.

He marked out the line of bulwarks he wished to create and began to search the headland for a suitable site to build a more substantial dwelling then his willow tree withy.

Finally, he settled on a bluff of land in the lee of the main headland, facing towards the lake of tidal waters. This had an uninterrupted view east and easier access to his furnace and to a view from the top of the site if danger threatened. This gave him greater command of the ground.

There was a more pressing practical reason too, for choosing this place. Here stood a small stand of oaks which he could fell on site, to build a more structured dwelling with a hardwood frame of oak with clunchstone, mud, and straw inter-filling for the walls. All of these materials could be brought from the side of the headland where they just needed to be dug and gathered from a seam of clay which he had discovered in the underbelly of the hillside when exploring his domain. Everything that he needed could be found close at hand. He drove flint wedges into the lengths of the felled timber to split the trunk and to give him the framework for his planned structure. He split and spliced the oak trunk until he had fashioned enough lengths of timber for his purpose.

His mare, as willing as ever, helped to haul the logs into position. Now, Henge realised that the heavy work he was asking of his mare, must cease. If she was to deliver a healthy foal for Lord Orris, much less must be asked of her than the mauling work he had demanded these past few days. Now he must be patient and await the return of the Tambour troupe from the West.

For the first time since the Summer Solstice, Henge had paused in his labours. In a moment of respite, he thought longingly of his bride to be. Would she remember him and long for him as he longed for her? He wondered whether the colt that he had gifted to her would be tamed by a gentle touch and bring much delight. Most of all, he hoped that the man who had given her the horse would remain a bright memory.

Then his time of ease was over, for Henge knew that the summer shoals of blue striped fish would soon pass by his headland home and must be gathered in the most bountiful catch of the year. He had learnt that by hanging his catch at the top of the furnace chimney, that the smoked fish could be stored for later, and began to set up racks at the top of the funnel to preserve what he could of them.

CHAPTER TWO - A DISTURBING ENCOUNTER

Now the skylarks had left their nests and Henge could harvest the rich grass, that had been created from the lark droppings, to help feed his mare for the winter. One day, as he laboured at his task, a boy stood by the line of green hawthorn twigs that had been planted earlier in the summer.

He paused at his task and spoke to the youth.

"Hello, young man. Have you come to watch me in my labours? I'll give you some fish if you help tie the grass into bundles."

The boy came forward and silently began to gather the grass as he was instructed.

Henge was surprised by this eagerness to help, but did not pause again in his labours. By the time the sun had reached its zenith, Henge headed towards the shade of a willow tree and produced a pitcher of water and two smoked fish, which he shared with this unexpected helper.

He gauged that the boy was about twelve and seemed hungry. He reminded Henge of his own youth when his father had died, leaving him to look after his mother and sister. He hesitated to enquire more of the boy at that moment. After all, what was he to do? Did he want to take on a child when his own survival had once seemed so precarious?

"What's your name, lad?" He asked now.

The boy hung his head in shyness, tongue-tied.

"You have worked well for me today. Come boy. Don't be shy. I am pleased with you. Well done!"

"Minos." The lad whispered.

"Well, Minos. If you want to come tomorrow to help me, I will give you two fishes. Do you have anything to exchange other than your labour? I also have fresh fish for you to take away. Where do you live?"

The boy was silent. "Come now, I won't hurt you!"

Minos pointed towards the west and said briefly. "I am with the potters."

"Oh yes, I know where they live. Do you have any pots to exchange for fish?"

"Well." The boy hesitated, twisting his feet together around his leg. "Maybe."

"Don't worry for the moment. I shall give you the fish I promised for your work today. I can give you two more tomorrow, if you want to help me."

The boy nodded, and Henge was left feeling he had understood the youngster. Well, he would see what happened next, for he was drawn by the eagerness that the child had shown in his day's work.

He admitted to himself, that any help would be useful at the moment, for he felt driven to prepare the headland for a more ambitious future.

By the time that the day's work was done, Henge was impressed by the work they had accomplished, and saw the youngster slowly retreat to where those potters shaped their wares.

As the youth slowly disappeared, watching him, Henge wondered. What was it about the boy that made him so appealing?

The next morning, the boy came early carrying a cooking pot.

"I see that you have taken me at my word. What a wonderful pot. Did you make it? Or was it made by your father?"

The boy shook his head but made no comment.

Henge did not press him but was surprised at his reticence.

Another day of harvest and sunshine but by the next day thunder clouds had gathered. However, the boy still arrived, willing to work.

"Perhaps you would like to help me give my horse some care. I have worked her hard this summer and now must take more care of her as she will have a foal next spring. If we are lucky."

The boy's face lit up, but still he was silent.

"Just remember, you must not get behind her, for she may kick or buck. If you talk gently to her, she will be a friend. Now bring her some fodder and water and we will give her a brush down."

Together they worked at brushing her coat with straw. Henge looked sadly down at her forelocks for her hooves were ragged. He remembered the skins of the fish that he had smoked, had been very oily and decided to wrap them over the hooves. Perhaps they would nourish them as they seemed to do for his own fingers after working at the furnace.

The rainclouds had cleared by the time that the boy left. Henge set his fish lines once more. He wondered where the boy went but continued the work of gathering in his catch and baiting hooks.

That evening remained calm. All sign of rain chased away, as the sun set over the distant hillside. Henge was tempted to bathe in the returning tide. For a brief moment, he was at leisure and peace and allowed the incoming tide to wash over him.

The help that the boy had given that day had left him with an evening of unusual calm and tranquillity of soul. He lay naked on the beach for the dying sun to dry his young body, and for a while he slept.

But his dreams were not the dreams of a lover but were peopled by violence and anxiety. Awaking to darkness, his body was chilled by the night air. And he hurried to put on his jerkin. Then, disturbed by the nature of the dream, he headed along the beach to banish the echoes of his sleep.

As he walked, all was quiet except the gentle lapping of the tide on shingle which comforted and calmed his soul. Now heading back to his willow withy, he climbed to the sand dunes and there heard a mumbled voice and chattering of teeth from somewhere amongst the sedge grasses. Following to where the sound was coming from, he almost fell over the reclining body of a child, there in front of him. "What the...Minos! What are you doing here? Where are your parents? They must be frantic that you have not returned home!"

"I don't...have...any parents. I am all alone now!"
He managed to say between gulps of air.

"What do you mean?" Asked Henge, now gripped
by an almighty anguish for he saw in this young
man, his own story.

"I haven't got...anyone...to worry about me." He
choked, swallowing his tears, at the same time
edging away warily.

Henge took a step forward, but the boy slid away
from him, out of arms reach. He saw the
instinctive cringe and recognised the boy's fear.
For hadn't it been his own reaction to occasional
beatings, without a father to defend him.

He paused, then abruptly he sat down on a hillock
in the sand dune. "Now. Now. There is no need to
fear me, lad. I am not going to hurt you. Don't you
know that I have been very glad of your company
these last few days. We worked well together,
didn't we? Come. Sit here, out of the fresh wind.
You will soon be chilled. Here, in the shelter of that
larger hillock." Henge said kindly.

"You have done me a good turn these last few days, for my duties have been many and your arrival on my headland home, came at just the best moment. So, I am concerned, that you should not suffer on my behalf. Now tell me. Is there no one to look after you?"

The boy shook his head, reluctant to admit his piteous state.

Henge wondered what to ask the boy, for he was obviously very frightened "you said, that you came from the potters' encampment."

Was that true? Did you steal the pot you gave me?" Henge persisted.

"No. No, I didn't. It was my mother's." He stopped, unwilling to say more.

They sat together in silence for a few minutes.

Henge could see how painful it was to perhaps admit that his parents were dead. He was caught in a dilemma. He did not wish to appear to have stolen the boy, if he had run away from home, but the boy was clearly in need of some help.

Even here, in the middle of summer, sharp breezes could blow off the big water. Henge certainly knew that. Hadn't he arrived here himself at this time of the year. He was tempted to take the boy to the furnace in the cliffside. That would certainly keep him from the cold night air. But Henge was reluctant to divulge the secret he had been keeping, with his stories of sea monsters and dragons. Then he thought of the natural way that that the boy had bonded with his black mare and suggested.

"Well, Minos, perhaps you will tell me more of your story sometime. Right now, I am beginning to feel very cold, so I am sure you are too. If you want to follow me back to my withy and horse's stable, I am sure I could find you some better shelter than these sand dunes."

"You've made friends with her already, haven't you?" The boy nodded vigorously.

At that, Henge stood up and ignoring the boy's scanty attire, he turned towards his own shelter and allowed the youngster to make his own mind up.

Henge urgently wanted to allow the boy to make his own decision. He knew how painful his own childhood had been and he did not wish the child to feel enslaved. No, his own experience of slavery, had been brief but still he was not about to impose this upon such a willing hand.

So, marching across the newly cut field of old skylarks' nests, they came to the riverside's inland lake and turned towards the lee of the headland where his withy and horse barn were situated.

Knowing that the boy had followed him across the open field, Henge dived into his shelter and brought out a flaxen sheet and his goatskin cloak. It was a mark of his trust that he gave this to Minos.

"Here, this will cover the straw for a bed for the night, and this goatskin coat I am entrusting to you, to keep you warm until we can get you something of your own. This is not a gift, for it is my most treasured possession, given to me for my first act of bravery in the chase. It is the best I can do until the morning, when we might build a shelter for you, if you decide to stay, that is?"

"For now, make yourself as comfortable as you are able, for I am tired of my labours and have much more work to do in the morning." With that, he left the boy there. Free, free to steal his precious cloak or take shelter with a young master who would treat him kindly. The choice was for Minos to make. To Henge, who had known all such terrors and hardships, it was important that the boy knew upon what terms they would live together.

Whatever the future held for them both, he would not break that bond of Minos' freedom. Fiefdom, he might earn, but never enslavement, for he knew to his own cost, what that had meant for the sister and brother born of the Circle of Stones Tribe.

CHAPTER THREE – MINOS TELLS HIS STORY

Earlier in the summer.

Just before the Spring Equinox to the North of the headland, in a deep valley that nestled into the hillside of Littledown, smoke lazily curled into the sky. It was a fine day and the air was still. All the potters were expecting to see the results of their labours as the kiln had been fired up and now all they needed to do was to wait for the fire to die down before seeing which pots had survived the intense heat.

Beako, the chief potter, was issuing orders to his underlings.

"Hurry up, you lazy scoundrels" He barked impatiently. He was due to take all the new pots to the Gathering at the other side of the river ford later that day, and he was in a hurry. The elderly man who was slowly attending to the kiln heard him. Beako's fit of rage was getting louder, and he knew the potter's temper was short.

The boy Minos, who was still in his hut at the top of the valley, could hear his father being chastised, and he sighed, before attending to their breakfast. He knew how hard his father worked but there was never any pleasing Beako. His father made the best pots in the community, but it was Beako who sold them at the Gathering, so there was no profit unless the big man returned with an empty cart.

He had begun to prepare their simple meal, when high above the valley Minos heard the sound of crashing crocks. Then an awful scream of pain which turned into a pitiful squeal before silence reined again. Then the sound of Beako shouting, incandescent with rage, came quite clearly to his ears.

"You fool. Look what you have done! Get up, clumsy clod! That's a week's worth of firings you have there in the kiln. What Bl---y fu--ing sloppiness!"

"Help me... I..."

"Here, Fredi. Pull him free, but be careful not to do any more damage as you move that worthless piece of excrement!"

The big man had turned away, rage clearly to be seen, bloating his cheeks with anger.

A few minutes before, the injured man's son was preparing their breakfast on hot stones at the top of the village. He heard a commotion below in the valley but kept his eyes on the pancakes he was preparing.

"Minos, Minos. Come quickly. Your father has had an accident." A small boy had cried outside their bothy.

As Minos had begun to run down the hill fearfully, the other two men at the scene of the accident, had unceremoniously pulled his father, foot first from the scene of devastation. Indeed, many pots were ruined amongst the remnants of the kiln. Then taking a half-filled bucket of water, the big man had unceremoniously flung it over the boy's injured father.

Some of the women looked on dispassionately at the man and one of them said. "Well. He's a goner, for sure." And she put a piece of hopsack over his head. Then she turned to Minos who was running down the hill. "Say goodbye to your father. He won't last more than a few minutes." And she turned away, no thought to comfort the youngster.

Well, that had been four turns of the moon ago and since that time, Minos had sought to help the potters in whatever way that would earn him a crust. But he was always hungry and no one else seemed to care about him.

Then, one day, Beako had been busy with a branding iron and Minos now realised that the big man intended to make him a slave. He called to his two helpers to bring Minos to him but realising what was about to happen, the boy ran up the hill and kept on running until he came to the Spring. No. He would not become a slave. Hadn't his father emphasized that they were all freemen at the Pottery Encampment. He had remembered.

He had decided to follow the stream down towards the midday sun and discover another home. He would rather kill himself than be Beako's slave, and all that implied.

Then, he had just put one foot in front of the other and walked towards the bright blue sky and the sun, into the freshening fragrant breeze that blew onto his overheated body.

Suddenly, wonder of wonders, Minos came upon a delightful sight! A great expanse of water sparkling in the sunlight, as far as the eye could see. It took his breath away and he rested there for a few minutes.

Seeing nothing but the sparkling waves, he had decided to walk to where the land jutted further out into the big water. Soon he came to a big field next to the headland and rested again, marvelling at the bright view in front of him. High above his head, larks carolled and on the grass was a lone figure reaping the long fragrant meadow. How sweet it all seemed after the sadness of his existence since his father had died. Now he rested again and chewed on a piece of grass, for by now he was very hungry.

Then, the man came over and offered him payment for his help. Two smoked blue fishes if he helped to stack the long grass into stooks.

CHAPTER FOUR – SUMMER DAYS AND THE MEETING AT THE GATHERING

It was now full summer and all the materials for Henge' new building were gathered onto his proposed site. He had cut sycamore and spruce and had again split these into thin planks which he had overlapped into panels. They had together gathered river reeds into bundles and left them in stooks to dry by the riverbanks. Soon he would raise a roof but left this so that the timber could be tempered for a while before the worst of the winter came.

The boy was proving to be an eager helpmate and even showed Henge how to mix the clay they had dug, with ash from their furnace to seal spaces where knots were found in the wood. Minos showed Henge how to dig a pit in the floor of the proposed house with runnels to allow air inside to increase the efficiency of the firepit. Then they enclosed this with large flat stones from the beach to be used as surfaces for the cooking pots. These could also be used for the making of flatbread when the stones were hot enough.

All these events were gradually explained to Henge. Minos life with the potters was where they must always deal with the safety of their fire, but there were always accidents happening. Henge realised that the cooking pot that Minos had given him, had been his most treasured possession, for it had been his mother's.

She had gathered herbs and seaweed, and wild carrot and river rhyzomes to put into the pot with barley or oats to make a potage. Sometimes, when they were available, shellfish or fish might be included. Even a sea bird could be added, if they were lucky.

Minos told of these things in the evenings when labour was done. Henge had pieced together a sorry tale from the snippets of information the boy had divulged. It seemed that his mother had died when he was much younger, he didn't quite know how long ago, but was when some of the river had iced over and many of the potters had also died with not enough food to eat. After that, his father had looked after him. But this summer, his father had fallen into the fire over the pottery kiln pit. Although rescued, he was badly burned and died soon after. This had meant that Minos now was all alone, and he had been made to fetch and carry big pots around the camp for scraps of food from the evening meal. If he was tired, they would beat him, and he would go hungry to bed.

So, his life had proceeded for the last few full moons, but his last beating had been so severe, that he had resolved to leave. It was at that point that Minos had come onto the headland.

All this story had echoes of his own childhood, although Henge had not been treated so harshly, for his father had been a respected man of the tribe, but the hand to mouth existence had been very similar. Now as he had learnt to survive, so he taught Minos, helping him to set traps and to gather mushrooms, being careful to teach the boy which were poisonous.

So, the weeks after the Summer Solstice were spent and the Autumn equinox was drawing near. For Henge, they were some of the happiest days of his young manhood. He was living in a dream of young love, working towards the time when his bride-to-be would return. The addition of the young boy as a summer companion was made even sweeter by the knowledge he could impart to this boy, an understanding of his place in the world, displaced and alone. Henge knew how that felt and he spent many hours teaching the boy how to survive.

He had never expected the lad to stay, but somehow, they suited each other. For a day's work, he was rewarded and his ability with looking after the mare had more than earned him his keep. But he was still a poor sight and Henge decided he must take a trip to the small gathering of sellers that came to a spit of land over the river, every few days. There he intended to barter for some clothes and bedding, to provide more than the rags the lad had come with.

They set off early and were soon at the Ford to the other side of the river. They had to wait for the tide to turn when the river would be at its lowest. It was pleasant to talk idly to others waiting there. After some while, Henge was engaged in conversation with a burly man with a bushy beard. He was a man of mighty height and muscles that rippled over his portly belly. He wore a thick hide bib, much stained by terracotta markings and seemed most agreeable. After some minutes of chatter about the weather and life in general, the man scratched his head. "Don't I know you from somewhere? Haven't I met you before? I don't usually forget a face."

Realising that this was probably one of the potters, Henge took time before he spoke. He carefully looked to where Minos was, but he was not in view. "Perhaps I have bought from you. I don't come to the stalls very often. I only come when I have fish to sell. What are you selling?"

The man made a loud guffaw. "What, you don't know 'Beako'? I am well known here for my beautiful pots. Best pots from all around!" He asserted.

"Ah. Well then, I might have bought some of them. Are you the potters from up near Thistlebarrow on Littledown? I bought a pitcher from them once. Good one too." Thinking to praise the man for his good workmanship whilst hoping the man would move on, for he was afraid that Minos would return whilst the man was still around.

"Yes, and by the stars in the sky, I have remembered. You must be the Bard, that lives amongst those sea creatures and dragons." He chuckled. "Best to keep nosy noses out of your way. Eh? I see your smoke burning every so often and it isn't just fish you are smoking, I'll be bound." He grinned and invited Henge to enlighten him.

At this, Henge began to be fearful that at any minute, Minos might appear. "Well, we all have to make a living somehow."

Turning aside he could see that the crowd was moving forward and he hastened away until the man was out of sight. Then ahead, his black horse could be seen moving with the flood of people over the shallow water now exposing the stones at its bed.

He hastened to catch up with his horse as he bobbed up in front of him between the heads of the gathered crowd. "Minos wait, I'm here." He shouted, trying to catch up and eventually he made the crossing and caught up with the boy. "Minos, it's alright. I know why you are so frightened. Don't worry."

"Oh, Oh." The boy said, much distressed, fear all over his face. "I've seen him, I've seen the potter who beat me and, oh, oh" unable to carry on.

"It's alright. You have no reason to fear him now. You do not have to return to him if you don't want to. You do not have to fear him now." Henge repeated, trying to calm the boy

"Tell me, do you have a mark on you? A branding to say that you belong to him?"

"No, nooo! That is what I ran away from. He had no right, no right at all. My mother and father were free members of the tribe, but he would have made me a slave."

"You are absolutely sure about this? Are there any other of the potters who would speak for you?"

"Well, I don't know. They are all afraid of him and I don't know if they would confirm whatever he says." Minos said uncertainly.

"For the time being, just keep away from them and keep the mare well away from the crowds. I will make my exchanges at the fair as quickly as possible so be ready to go back home. Feed and water the mare and by then I should be ready."

Henge passed along the stalls until he found what he was looking for. A hopsack jerkin, a sheepskin and some stoat pelts. He hurried back to where he had left Minos with his horse but could not immediately see him. Then, straight ahead, he saw Beako conferring with some of the other potters who were pointing towards the willow by the river.

Too late, Henge saw that Minos was hiding the mare and knew that they were trapped.

He hastened towards Beako and in a loud voice hailed him." Friend, I am glad to have found you, for we were separated before. I wonder whether you have sold all your pots? I am looking for a beaker, stoutly made to put wild berries and crab apples in to keep for the winter."

"Well. I might have." Beako said, not able to pass up a sale and he turned to his barrow to sort through his goods. What about this one?" He said, a crafty look on his face.

"Mm. Perhaps?" Henge said uncertainly looking further into the barrow.

"But where's your mare? I thought he was with you earlier?"

Keeping his voice, a tone louder Henge said. "Oh, I promised a boy some fish if he would look after her for a while. Very willing he was. Well, what do I owe you for the pot?"

Beako beamed. "Oh, just one willing boy will do." He said, smiling triumphantly.

Henge glanced around and saw that quite a crowd had gathered. By the looks of them, potters all. "Oh really, well we better see about that. I don't think that boys are for sale in this market. Do you think anyone here has ever bought a child for sale?" He challenged those around to speak up.

"Look around. Have any of the people here, heard of a child being bought at this market?"

They were all silent, not wishing now, to be involved.

"Perhaps we should ask the boy himself whether he wants to come to you. What will you pay him.?

"Pay him! That lazy good for nothing!"

"Oh. So, you know him already? Perhaps it was you he was running away from when I first saw him. Poor wretch, he was. He looked half-starved and covered in lash marks. Your doing, where they, eh.?"

By now, there was quite a crowd.

"Come on! Give me the boy!" Shouted Beako, stepping forward menacingly.

Henge stood his ground. "I don't think so." Facing the big man sturdily. "Come here, boy. I will not harm you and I won't hand you over to this man. Now. Is this the man you ran away from when your father died?"

The boy walked forward, leading the mare, clutching tightly to his reins. "Yes." He managed in a small voice.

"Do you want to go back with him to the Potters Encampment?"

Minos shook his head.

"Come now, you will need to speak up for the good folk must hear you clearly as I ask again. "Do you want to go back to the Potters Encampment?" Henge said in ringing tones. "To be beaten and ill-used now that your father is dead? Do not fear. I shall not sell you to this man for one small urn."

"No." Minos said in a clear piping voice.

"And do you wish to work with me on my headland, as you have been doing for the past cycle of the moon?"

"Yes. Yes!" Said the boy as loudly as he could muster.

"Then the matter is settled." Said Henge looking hard at Beako and all the bystanders. "It seems I have no use for your urn, after all. Another day, perhaps?" He said firmly, challenging this big bully to waylay him, as he took the boy's hand and tossed his purchases onto the mare's saddle, then he took the reins from Minos. For a second, Beako stood his ground, but then fell back and let him through the crowd that had witnessed the event.

"I'll be seeing you." Beako called back to them as they left the circle of bystanders behind.

"Well, I hope that is settled for a while, but I don't think that will be the end of the matter. Hop up here, on the horse's back and hang on to me for I think it best to hurry." Henge said to the frightened boy, who was almost paralyzed with fear. They progressed silently, then Henge said. "Before we leave the river completely, I would point out that hill on the other side of the ford, between the two rivers. The leader of that hill Tribe is a friend of mine. If there is any trouble, do you think you could find your way there? It would mean crossing the river again to reach it?"

"I think so." Said the boy uncertainly.

"Good lad! That is all I can expect of you, but it is always best to anticipate any trouble before it starts." He said bracingly, but deep down, knew that he had made an enemy and was full of foreboding.

CHAPTER FIVE - TROUBLE AT THE FIVE RIVERS TRIBE

Meanwhile, Lord Orris and those that had travelled with him to the Solstice celebrations at the Roundwood Gathering, where Henge had exchange pledges with his bride to be, had returned to their home to find the place in turmoil.

Lucca's punishment at the hands of the Roundwood Tribe for stealing Henge' colt, was meted out according to Forest laws. He had been whipped, then chased out into the forest night and had been heading East in disgrace. But when the morning sun rose again, his fears of the dark forest night were dispelled, and he had doubled back and northwards to further up-stream of the river.

By this time, his anger and outrage at Henge's outwitting his intended steal of his black colt, had turned from fear of the forest, to resolve to arrive at his Tribal encampment before Lord Orris returned. In this way he had reached Alderwood, well ahead of the other party of travellers from the Roundwood Gathering.

Several of the Elders had chosen to stay away from the Solstice Gathering and had been expressing open rebellion to Lord Orris' leadership. Many of them wished to change the way of doing things, for the days of relying on game to feed them was coming to an end.

More of the tribes had chosen to leave the nomadic life and had begun to sow the land with barley and wheat, and gathered upland grass to feed their animals and livestock to overwinter them. So far, the Five Rivers Tribe had been content to keep to the old ways. The famine of eight winters before, had seen the death of many of the young children. These would have grown to be the young blood of the tribe, the next generation of hunters.

But this had not happened, and the Elders wanted to make their encampment, a more settled one. They had found a valley with a reliable stream which had undulating gentle-sided slopes. There were stands of oak to shelter them from the occasional harsh winds, and the land was fertile and took their plough easily. A bit stony, perhaps, but grew a good early grass to feed their horses.

Now they had planned to plant grain on some of the gentler slopes and had decided to build more permanent groups of buildings in the heart of the valley.

By the time that Lord Orris returned to the Encampment, the Elders had listened to Lucca's version of events that twisted the news to be more favourable to his own grievance. The tribal Elders had by now decided to replace Lord Orris with Lucca as their new leader. And he was there to meet the travellers as they returned.

The two men looked at each other. Lord Orris, in some surprise said loudly. "Why Lucca, I am surprised to see you here so soon. I thought at least you would hide away to cover your shame. Horse stealing is a serious offence. Have you told the Elders what happened? No doubt your version of events!"

Not in the least abashed by Lord Orris' words, Lucca sneered. "There you are, Orris. Showing your preference for that no-good spinner of tales, Henge. Yes, I did tell them that he was there at the Gathering. It seems to me he confirmed my estimation of him. Full of lies, he was, with his tales of Sea Serpents and Dragons.!"

"You couldn't trust anything he had to say. I was only testing out his colt, with a mind to buy. I wasn't given a chance to defend myself when you were so busy with mating his mare with your stallion. You got it all wrong, and I was made to suffer great humiliation at his hands. I shan't forget that in a hurry!"

Lord Orris crossed his arms over his chest. Oh, what a liar this man was. Why had he not seen this when Lucca had persuaded the council to banish Henge five years before. He thought. But this time he could not hide from the truth. His own jealousy of his wife's affection for someone else. He did not then know that it was brotherly love. So, he had allowed himself to be persuaded to agree to the banishment. To rid himself of a rival! Well, now he only had himself to blame! He thought.

Lucca interrupted his thought. "You are getting old, Lord Orris, and the Elders think the same. Don't you men?" He asked in ringing cheer. "It has been decided that I should take over the leadership from now on. After all, you have other responsibilities now, haven't you?" He mocked, referring to his wife's fragile state of mind.

Orris looked around at all the hunters, and there was no sign of disagreement from them.

"Do you all agree that Lucca should be your Leader? A liar and a cheat. Condemned by all that were gathered at the Summer Solstice. This man, who is vicious and self-serving."

He looked around at them all, not quite believing that they could be so foolish, but they all stood around, some looking guiltily at their feet. But none of them raised any objection.

"So be it!" He said harshly, accepting defeat.

Then Lucca came forward and in smug tones said. "After all, Orris, we all make mistakes, don't we? You should have killed that boy when you had the chance. When you made your own decision to raid the Stone Circles Tribe in the year of the famine. Thieves and murderers, you made us all then, so why are you so high and mighty now?" Lucca mocked.

"It is the survival of the tribe that matters, and you are no longer fit to lead it. You are getting too old and foolish for that honour. I shan't let any other tribe walk over me again, don't' you worry."

With this rallying call, some of the hunters cheered. But not all. Some of them hung their heads in shame at their own pusillanimity!

By now, it was late evening and the returning travellers went their separate ways to reorganise their baggage. Nothing more was said that night, and it was only the reassuring loving from the Lady Raisa that gave Lord Orris back his sense of worth. That he was not needed here was clear. But did he feel able to stay here under these changes. Would the 'old bull' be able to accept the ascendency of a new hunter? It was now time for reflection.

******

July passed for Lord Orris and the Lady Raisa in pleasures of the simplest kind. Taking delight in each other's company and learning the secrets of more intimacy. Mother Ava saw this with the greatest satisfaction for she had grieved mightily at their estrangement. The Lady Raisa saw that her role as wife as well as mother was to heal the deep hurt that Lucca had inflicted by his treachery. Freedom for Lord Orris from his duties, was an opportunity for them to delight in each other. For once, their son was not the complete focus of his father's attention, and it was for Mother Ava to keep him occupied.

By the next repeat of the moon's cycle, the harvest was beginning to ripen, and their hopes were centred on this. If this was not satisfactory, then the hunters would need to use those skills that they had neglected.

Traps were set to catch the fish returning to the sea and they looked for new off-springs of deer and wolf, beaver, and otter. The wild boar began to forage for storm-shed acorns under the canopy of oaks, but worms and grubs must satisfy them until more nuts had ripened.

All the tricks of survival must now be used to gather all of nature's bounty to store for the winter.

Raisa was learning many of the secrets of nature from Mother Ava, for she would need to know the benefits of all the bounty to be found. Blackberry and crab apple, rosehips and Hoars, Blueberries and Raspberries, all needed to be processed for winter storage, and the women of the tribe had this duty. Ancient cures for ailments were gathered to help them through bad times and accidents. Lavender and Sage, Peppermint and Parsley, all found their way into the winter stores.

If he was grieving for his responsibilities, Orris did not show it, for he was deeply content to see Raisa so much happier and was comforted by her response to his needs. Time slipped by gently in the warm summer weather.

Then, in the middle of the next phase of the moon, before the equinox red moon of autumn, came an urgent messenger from the Riversmeet Tribe. Henge was at serious threat from the Beaker people who made pots at Thistlebarrow Down.

It was time for action!

Henge crested the hill after showing Minos the way to the hill tribe's encampment. He was still full of foreboding.

He thought that Beako would not take his refusal lightly, but Henge resolved to keep his word to the boy.

Turning south, the headland stretched away in front of him and on the wind came a distinct smell of burning. Henge halted and strained to see ahead.

Over the flat expanse of grassland, newly cut, and towards the river, a sudden flash of fire. His withy home? He strained to see more clearly but his instinct told him, this was the work of Beako. Their own delay had allowed the potter to be ahead of him.

"It seems your potter master is determined to pick a quarrel with me, Minos. Do you see where my house is on fire?"

"He can't do that!" Said the boy, fiercely. "I must stop him." Urging the horse forward.

"Hey, steady. It's no use, the fire is well alight and we need help with this fight. Do you remember the road I have just shown you, to the hill tribe?"

"Yes." Said Minos.

"Well, do you think that you could run as fast as you can, to the ferryman, who will take you across the river. Henge took the goatskin off his arm and from his belt drew a dagger and cut two small pieces of the fur pelt.

"Take these, one for the ferryman and one for the Chief of the tribe called Tarsus. Chief Tarsus." He repeated. "Can you remember that?"

The boy nodded uncertainly. "But I ought to help you here." He pleaded.

"You will help most by doing what I say." Henge said firmly, a note of steel in his voice. Come! Time is pressing. Will you do as I ask? Are you able to do what I ask of you? Come, give me your answer."

The boy slid off the back of the horse, clutching the two pieces of goatskin and ran swiftly away down the hill to the river.

* * * *

The Five Rivers Encampment. Same night.

Whilst Henge was facing his greatest peril, Lord Orris was at his most perplexed. If he was grieving for his responsibilities to the tribe, he did not show it, for he was deeply happy in his loving of the Lady Raisa and her responses to his needs.

Time slipped by gently in the warm summer weather. In the middle of the next phase of the moon, the last before the Equinox red moon of autumn, there came an urgent messenger from the hill tribe, between the two rivers. Henge was at serious threat from the Beaker people who made pottery at Littledown. It was time for action!

Hengistbury Head. The evening before.

Henge kicked his heels into his mare's flanks and cantered over the greensward but towards his smoking furnace. Just before the clifftop, he turned east until he came to a small rise in the ground, at the foot of the escarpment. He flung himself off the horse and tethered her behind a small bush.

Then he felt for his dagger and fell to the ground where he began to dig away at the earth, until he heard a clink of metal. He redoubled his efforts and soon retrieved, very carefully, a fine sword from the soil.

Now, following the line he had marked out for his defences, crept up to the burning hut where he could hear the excited cackle of men's voices – one, two, three. He counted. Yes, Beako and two less sturdy fellows.

Coming upon them, from the other side of the burning willow withy, he slashed two half burnt slender branches still alight, with his sword. Grabbing them by the still unburnt end, he swung this around his head in a wide circle and advanced on the two lesser miscreants in this act of arson.

"Get away, Get away. You miserable curs! This fight is between Beako and me. This is not your quarrel, but if you assist him further, by all the powers of the heavens, I swear I will kill you all!"

They stepped back, unwilling to tackle this flashing fury, fire and steel at the ready.

"Oh, so you want a fight, do you. Eh?" Said Beako, advancing from the other side with an even bigger burning branch which had the power of a cudgel. But Henge had seen the log and felt the heat, and sidestepping, whipped his own willow around Beako's ankles. The forward movement of the bigger man, was temporarily arrested and he fell forward heavily onto the flaming log. With a scream of pain, Beako rolled away from the searing heat and held his hand to his face.

"You've blinded me." He squealed.

"Get this man to the sea to cool him off." Said Henge, now sickened by the result of the potters' violence. "I shan't forget this day's work Beako, and may you also remember this act of vengeance against me. Know that this land belongs to me, The Bard of Hengistbury Hill, and whoever seeks sanctuary here, will be defended. I shall fight to the death to keep what I have made of this headland."

One of the two men with the blinded fireraiser, both potters, said. "So be it. We will keep our word to stay away, but I don't think that he will be troubling you again in a hurry."

They helped the stricken, whimpering man to his feet, to tend to his wound. As they left, Henge was suddenly overcome by the visceral hatred that he had felt, at their violation of his home.

There would be nothing left of the withy, but ashes. He sat there, watching the flames consume all that had been wrest from the last five years work. Except, he now remembered, for the mare. He jumped up. He must make sure that she was safe. Perhaps, in return, she would accept him as an uninvited guest? He thought wryly.

Henge had fed and watered his mare but had stayed by the remnants of his home until all was consumed. The blackened stump of the willow tree, was all that remained. He had meant to join his animal in the shack, but had fallen asleep under the stars, in the shelter of bramble bushes, for the night was calm and the moon had glowed in the heavens, belying the violence that had been done this night.

Somehow, it had given him comfort and the next thing he knew, was the sound of a piping voice and a deeper one coming nearer as dawn broke through cloud.

"Oh, Oh. What has happened. How awful! Where is Henge? I should have stayed to help him. Oh!" The piping voice said on a sob.

"No. No. You did the right thing. He sent you as a messenger. For you would not have been able to stop this fire. This was very thoroughly lit from all sides, to have burnt so completely." The voice of

Chief Tarsus said. "But I fear for Henge, nevertheless. Where is he?"

"I'm here." Croaked a voice from the lea of a bramble bush nearby, and Henge rose unsteadily from his shelter.

"By the stars! Are you alright? What has happened to you?" Asked Chief Tarsus as he rushed to help the stricken man.

"It is no matter. Just stiffness, I think." Henge replied, still in a very strange voice. The only sign of the trauma of the night.

"Who did this to you? Come, take my cloak. You must be chilled through. How monstrous! To burn down a man's home." Tarsus continued. "Who were they?" He pressed for an answer, anger breaking through in his voice.

Henge began to laugh in a strange way, but crumpled up at their feet in a fit of coughing.

"Here boy. Help me to take Henge away from here. You can see, the man is hurt. But what of his horse? His stable still stands. Look! Even his mare is still here."

"My Cloak, my goatskin cloak." Henge whispered.

Minos, looked in the shack and stroked the mare, who was much agitated by the odd sound of their voices.

"Oh beauty. Are you alright?" He said to the horse, stroking her neck. "It's Minos here. You know me, don't you." He saw, there in the corner of the stall, the animal skin all laid out with the purchases of yesterday. The new sheepskin on top of them all.

He snatched up the goatskin and took it to warm his master who was now sitting on a small hillock with Chief Tarsus sitting anxiously beside him. "Good lad! Here, put this round your shoulders. You will soon feel better." He said, talking to Henge.

"Now, 'Minos.' Is that your name?" He asked. The boy nodded his head, his anxiety for Henge, evident. "Could you find something to carry some water from the river? I think a drink might help."

Minos snatched up the leather horse bucket and turned to fetch the water. As he passed the blackened withy, there beside the willow stump, was the pitcher that Henge had first exchanged for fish on his visit to the potters' camp, years before.

"Look, Henge!" Minos exclaimed. "My father's pitcher! My father's work! It is still here and I think, still usable." Moving to rescue the pot from the ashes.

"Be careful! The fire might still be burning." Warned Tarsus. But the boy had already snatched up the jug and fled to the river to give his master a drink.

He as quickly returned with the water in each container, but in his haste, without first washing the pitcher out, and the water was mixed with all the ashes from the fire!

At this, Henge who had recovered a little, let out a feeble laugh, and croaked "Nay, Minos, if the fire didn't kill me then the ash surely will!" And he took a great draft of water from the horse's bucket.

Mortified, the boy snatched up the pitcher again and fled to the river.

Then Tarsus turned to Henge and asked urgently. "What was this all about?"

"I'm afraid I clashed with Beako the potter, at the river crossing. This boy had fled from his encampment after his father died earlier in the year. He appeared one day on the headland in a sorry state. But he seemed to be interested in what I was doing and I said he could have a smoked fish if he helped me gather up the hay. He was a shy little thing and it was after several days of appearing here and willing to help me in return for fish, that I learnt that he had run away from the potters' encampment after his father had died in their furnace."

"He had fled barbarous misuse by Beako who had attempted to brand him a slave. When the boy realised what his fate might be, he fled."

"I knew what that might mean, for I also had lost my father at his age and was much misused by our tribe afterwards. I offered him shelter and food in exchange for some work and he had been with me for a full change in the moon. He seemed very willing to help me, especially with my mare. But as you see, he was pitifully dressed and I resolved to purchase him some better clothes."

"We went yesterday to the fair across the river. Unfortunately, Beako, a potter, was there. The child was frightened excessively when he thought that the man would take him by force. He offered to buy the boy from me, for the price of a pot, thinking I had made him my property."

"I managed to gather a crowd to witness that the boy was not for sale and that he was able to come with me of his free choice. That he was not a slave to be bought and sold and that it was wrong of Beako to suggest such a transaction."

"Well, we left without harm, for there were many witnesses to the event, but I was very suspicious that I had made an enemy. With this in mind I had taken Minos to see where your encampment could be found. As we returned to our route and slowly made our way home, I saw the fire from a distance and knew that it was trouble with Beako."

"I knew the boy was the cause, for I had defied the potter and was anxious that the boy would be hurt by him. That Minos did just as I commanded him to do, was testament to his willingness to help me."

Henge fell silent. exhausted by all this talk. The boy came skipping back with the two containers, this time with the pitcher no longer smoke covered.

"There, is that better, Master? It was hard to remove all the soot but I think the water is clear. I am glad that the fire didn't take this pot." Said Minos, implying so much more than he expressed.

"Much better, Minos." Tarsus said heartily. And if you know where some smoked fish might be found we might perhaps break our fast.

Coming out of a reverie, Henge said. Oh. Young man, I forgot in all that has happened, that there is a small package in the mare's shack which was purchased for you yesterday. He said with a crooked smile, trying to rescue some small joy from all that had happened.

Early the next morning Lord Orris dressed and saddled his horse but the Lady Raisa was beside him before he was able to slip away. "What is this, My Lord?"

"Oh, nothing too alarming. But I have been sent word that your brother might need a hand."

"But why, so soon, and on your own?" She asked, realising that there was more to his preparations. He had dressed in a mantle and chest and arm protectors and on his saddle, she glimpsed his sword.

"What! Armed for trouble and alone?" She challenged him.

"Don't hinder me woman." He said crossly. "There is man's work to be done! But give me your kiss farewell." He asked touching her cheek.

"Dear Lord, gladly." She said, now much distressed but knew that she must not delay him for there was an urgency in his actions and she began to fear for her brother as well.

Then he dug his heels into his mount and clattered away from the encampment.

* * * *

"What is this? Asked Lucca, to the Lady Raisa as he came upon her. "Where is Lord Orris" He challenged her. "What business takes him away from the encampment and why was I not informed? My permission has not been sought. He, of all people, should know the rules. It is insolent to flout the customs of submission! Where has he gone? Answer me!"

"I don't know." Whispered Raisa, now alarmed at his tone. "He hasn't told me anything." Afraid, to tell him that it was something to do with her brother.

"H'm, well as soon as he returns, send him to me." And he turned on his heel and walked away, anger in every line of his body.

If Orris had realised his error, he would not have acted any differently for he would not submit to this usurper. It was concern for the rest of the tribe that had dictated his quiet demeanour during the past cycle of the moon, but underneath he was deeply troubled by this man's treachery.

All his actions since being at the Ringwood Gathering had seemed focused on his ongoing obsession about meeting Henge again.

On the Headland: -

Now, recovered a little, Henge went back to his story. "You will be glad to hear that after all this wrecking game, we will not hear much more from Beako, I think. I arrived at the height of the fire to find him and two miserable lackeys, enjoying their destruction." He paused, summoning up the strength to go on with his story.

"But by then, I was well prepared with a dagger at my waist and a sword in my hand.?"

"A sword in your hand you say?" Tarsus queried.

"Yes. You know me by my iron tools, but is not a sword but another tool. One I had learned to make, by a master craftsman who told me to bury them deep until the time of need. For he had come from a land across the sea where people use such weapons that he had crafted for them, to wage war on their fellow men. He knew that one day I would need to defend my life here on my headland."

Henge shook his head. Then continued. "By now, I was well prepared with a dagger at my waist and a sword in hand. I had cut two willow branches from the thatch which were well alight at one end only, all bendy and ablaze. I used these to scare off the two miserable curs that were helping Beako. Then he attacked, having first picked up a blazing log to use as a cudgel. Swinging round from his intended blow, I used the flaming willow to curl round his legs and trip him. As he went down, the burning log hit him in the eyes. By his own hand, he was blinded."

"I acted first in defence of my home, but then myself. For he would not have scrupled to beat me to death with his burning cudgel."

They were all silent, trying to imagine the scene. The boy spoke then. "You mean that I can stay with you forever...?" He asked earnestly.

The two men laughed at his simple request, more in relief at the outcome of the fight than at the boy. Then in a more serious tone. "You may stay as long as you wish, or unless, or unless." Henge hesitated. He did not wish to frighten the boy with what might not happen, then said. "Of course, you may stay. You are my horse's friend also, and how will I manage when she has her foal, eh?" Henge asked, seeking to steer the talk away from the deeds of yesterday.

The boy looked at the two men and was satisfied with the answer. But afterwards, Henge recalled the depth of wisdom in the boy's eyes. He had not been fooled about the possible further outcome of the confrontation. But 'sufficient unto the morrow'. He thought.

* * * * *

Lord Orris. North of the Riversmeet Tribe.

Orris rode briskly along the route he had taken two moons earlier. Along the high track, keeping the river to the left, he reached the encampment at the Roundwood turning. Instead of taking the path that fell steeply to the river crossing, he carried on westward until the lie of the slope fell away to a flat bogland. This was criss-crossed by brooks where the river he had been following, meandered into many different streams, over the valley floor. These finally came together again at the foot of a steep hill. This blocked the paths of the wayward streams until they reunited with the mother river. He saw this hill ahead and knew that it was the right way to the headland of the big water, that Orris was seeking.

He began to climb again, to the hilltop, seeking Chief Tarsus. As he rode into the midst of the encampment, a youth approached him.

"Well, My Lord, I am glad to see that you arrive so promptly. My father, had left for the headland of your friend, The Bard. Last night, a poor boy brought news that Henge was under attack and that his dwelling was burning. I have no more news than that. As you can imagine, my father hastened to assist his friend. I know nothing more, but he has not returned."

"H'm. This doesn't sound good, if it was necessary to send a boy for help. Perhaps you could spare someone to direct me to the crossing over the river. Then I follow the river, don't I?"

"Yes. That's right. You won't get lost if you follow the far side bank of the river. At a certain point there is a ford that you can cross, but I think you will have to wait awhile for the right state of the tide. I should say, that it should take you about one hour. I will come with you to the far side of the hill to point the way."

"Thank you, my friend!"

They progressed along a ridge until coming to a view of the two rivers converging on the plain below, with a misty horizon, overlooking a large expanse of blue water, as far as the eye could see. They stopped and Chief Tarsus' son said.

"This is as far as you need my help. Follow the road to the mid-day sun and you will come to the river crossing and on to the headland. Good luck! I hope that you find that all is now well, after all. I, Dugo, son of Tarsus bids you farewell." And he turned away to their encampment.

Lord Orris watched him go, then turned to descend the slope down to the plain and river below. Where the first river that he had followed had sparkled with sunlight and friendly streams, this river appeared dark and deep, flowing more purposefully to the sea.

Once on the flat ground, he touched the horse's flank with his heels and followed the young man's instructions. Without tiring the horse, they soon came to the river. He saw that the tidal water was still high, but urged his horse into the flow and they swam across onto the western bank. A wide expanse of cut grass now lay in front.

What a lovely piece of ground. He thought. But to his horror, ahead could be seen the blackened remnants of a small hut, but no one there.

Swinging off his horse to see what had happened, he called, in anguish. "Henge, Henge, are you here." But there was no answering shout.

He saw an abandoned horse bucket and looked for the mare, seeing the unscathed shack for the horse but no animal. Seeing that the withy had been destroyed he feared to find Henge dead amongst the ashes, but nothing was there to alarm him further.

Orris looked towards the sea and could make out the beginnings of a larger structure in progress. He moved towards this and saw some movement ahead, and his hopes rose. Hurrying across the open space he saw Henge moving among the skeleton of this new building. Next, a young boy could be seen and then he recognised Chief Tarsus.

"Henge." Orris shouted, and hurried to cross the uneven rough hillocky ground. Coming closer, he was shocked to see the state of his friend.

Blackened and grave of face. Lines of anxiety were clearly to be seen on the young man's face.

Lord Orris' instinct had been to hug the young man that he remembered, as he was in the month of the solstice. But the man in front of him, had changed in some indefinable way. The light had gone from his eyes and a distant look had hardened and ravaged his jawline. Henge nodded, in acknowledgement of Lord Orris. "You came." He said, no warmth in his greeting.

Orris looked to Chief Tarsus. "Hello. Thank you for the message. I came as soon as possible."

"I am glad you are here." Said Chief Tarsus. "You can see what has happened and we are assessing it. The withy is completely gone but no damage to the new structure has been done."

"What happened here. I have seen the destruction, but why and where are the villains?" Orris asked.

Chief Tarsus, looking for Henge to explain, saw his state and explained. "Well, it seems that, for the time being, there is no threat from that quarter because Beako, the potter, was a victim of his own aggression. He tripped during the confrontation with Henge, and fell onto a burning log that he was about to use as a cudgel and his eyes came into contact with the burning coals at its end and were severely burnt. Maimed certainly, but in my opinion, may still be dangerous."

Turning then to Henge, Orris asked. "And what of you, Henge? Are you alright? That is more important!"

"Oh. I'm well enough. I am still whole. I have my two arms and two legs. What else must I wish for?" He said in a strangled voice. It was clear that he was in a state of shock for it seemed that his heart had broken.

"I shouldn't expect any more in this life, should I? I shouldn't expect to be left alone to live my life without fear of interference. If I prosper on my windy outpost and make a life, half happy and in expectation of a loving wife and family. No, for the likes of me, the life of an outcast is all that I can expect, and I shouldn't have hoped for anything more." His voice had lost its hard edge and it trembled on the brink of breakdown.

Orris, with anguish in his voice said. "Dear boy, dear boy. Of course, you should, indeed you must. You have everything to live for. You have done so much already. Of course, you must expect these things. You will have them. We shall help you to succeed in your ambition." He longed to hug this man to him but saw that Henge was hanging onto reason by a thread.

Whilst he had been speaking, they had not been looking at the boy, Minos, who had been quietly listening and who then acted on instinct.

He went up to Henge and in a simple way, put his hand into Henge' hand and said quietly.

"But you are not alone now. You have me. I will look after you."

All was quiet, for his simple words and actions had struck just the right note. The weakest had come to help him, who had been the strongest.

Henge then fell to his knees and the two older men caught him before he toppled to the ground in total collapse.

They headed for the mare's shack with the deeply shocked Henge. He had been alone and guarding his territory for so long – five years since he had tried to live on this headland. The last complete cycle of the sun's 24 hours orbit had brought all his fears and hopes crashing around him and was finally at the end of his resources.

Then they laid him on the straw pallet which they covered with the sheepskin he had brought from the market the day before, and pulled his goatskin over him. They found the kirtle and linen cloak and seeing the state of the child, guessed that these were his purchases of yesterday and gave them to Minos to wear. Then set the boy to guard his master's sleep.

Chief Tarsus and Lord Orris set off for the beach to check the fish lines that Henge had set the day before. Two of his lines had broken away from their moorings, for the lateness of checking them meant that they were too heavily laden with their catch, and had torn away from their pegs. Two of the lines remained and they baited them up again and tossed them into the surf.

They walked along the beach towards the red stones and smelled the fire burning into the cliffs. Curious to find the source of the fire, they continued along the cliffs looking into the many indentations hewn by the action of the waves. To their amazement, they finally came to a deeper more cave-like hollow and came upon Henge' forge, carefully hidden by the formation of the rock.

"By Jove and all the Stars! Look what we have here! So, this is where Henge has been labouring to bring forth iron. How does he do it?" Asked Orris in amazement.

Tarsus Laughed. "Well. He certainly knew how to deter curious eyes. Why, he is the Bard of Henge' Headland of course! He had all these tales of sea monsters and dragons to keep his secret safe. Wonderful stories full of chilling images. He made sure that no one trespassed on his secret forge."

"But how did he make this metal appear? He certainly knew how to make not only tools but knives and even swords. I saw his sword with my own eyes. A fine sword. But how did he do it?" Puzzled Tarsus.

"Well, Mother Ava, the sage of my tribe, told us that he had been living with an old man who had been shipwrecked while seeking certain stones and knew the mysteries of these shoreline boulders that could be turned into such things. Together they had lived here for five years. He had taught Henge to make these goods and gave him the chance to prosper and make something of his life. But the old man had died at the time of the Spring Solstice and left Henge alone again on his windy headland."

Orris now was silent but had much to ponder. This was why Henge had no need to return to the tribe

– until now perhaps? For he had been completely self-sufficient.

His heart ached for his former slave child and the enormous burden he had carried all this time. He now understood why Henge had seemed so self-assured and powerful. He was physically a match for all comers. But at what cost? He now understood that the act of arson had been a huge shock, especially when it had been precipitated by his defence of the young lad.

Lord Orris now saw that the boy who was guarding Henge at the moment, was the same age that he had first known Henge. He could see that Minos had filled the aching hollow that his sister had left and which he, Orris had felt at the death of his own children who had died in the year of the plague. Henge had filled that void in his own life. The defence of the boy, had set Henge on a path with unexpected consequences. Now Orris saw that here was a way to make reparation for his own act of madness when his hunters had ravaged the Stone Circles Tribe, searching for food in the winter of blight across the land.

Orris turned to Tarsus. "Friend, I am indeed grateful that you warned me of what was happening here. I am even more aware of what your friendship to this young man meant to him. We are all carried by some invisible thread and here is one that I must not break."

"I intend to stay here until I can see some improvement in this remarkable human being's health. I know that you have many other responsibilities to your own people, but I think it is, perhaps, important to find out what is happening at the potters' encampment. It seems that Beako is damaged and may die, but if he recovers, will be very dangerous and stirring up more trouble."

"Yes, I was wondering about that too." Tarsus agreed. "I have to return to the hill but will try to find out what is happening at the potters' encampment. If danger threatens again, I will try to warn you. Do you want a message to be sent to the Five Rivers Tribe?"

"Perhaps to the Lady Raisa only. No more than, 'all is well.' But no mention of where I am or what I am doing. There are changes in my tribe and the miscreant that stole Henge' horse has stirred up trouble for me. In no circumstances do I want him to learn of Henge' troubles. He is a malicious man and would be more than happy to align himself with Beako."

"What trouble there is in this world!" Exclaimed Tarsus. "I shall do just as you say. Rest assured."

Orris bade Tarsus farewell and walked back to the only shelter, passing by the skeleton of the new building that Henge had planned. He saw all the hewn timber and the ground work that had already been completed. What an amazing amount of thought and energy had gone into the preparations for this building.

He stopped and inspected what had already been achieved. Here was a way, he thought thankfully, to bring Henge back from the brink of his despair. A new beginning – just as Henge had planned it! What other events had prompted this young man to start this project which Orris saw was very ambitious, after the life he had been living in his tree shelter?

Now he carried the catch of fish back to the charred remains of the withy. Looking around the shelter, he could not see any signs of any dry fish entrails and wondered whether Henge had baited an eel trap. Walking towards the river, he saw what he had guessed to be the case as he found a crude eel trap with several eels inside. He gutted the fish and dropped the entrails into the trap. Then returned to the burnt-out hovel to cook the cleaned fish.

Soon he had a small fire burning and his catch was ready. Skewered onto sticks, he now took the food to the shack.

Both the boy Minos, and his master were fast asleep and he wondered whether to leave them to sleep on.

He went to the lea of the shack where the mare and his horse were tethered. Stroking them, he whispered softly to his horse, then moved on to the mare. He ran his hand over the mare's belly and thought he found sighs of some enlargement. Was the mare pregnant? He hoped so for she was a fine animal and had been well cared for.

The rattle of the horse bucket and the slurping of the water had finally roused the boy who came to see to the feeding of the horses.

Minos stroked the mother softly, meanwhile talking in a gentle voice.

"She is a good mare, isn't she? You aren't afraid of her?" Orris asked.

"No. No. She is my friend and Henge relies on me to look after her." He said proudly.

Orris recognised the same willingness to work and eagerness to please, that he had seen in Henge and he breathed a sigh of relief. This boy would do much to heal his master and marvelled at the working of the spirit. "Good lad. I see you are ready to look after your master."

"You must understand that he is grieving for more than the burnt-out withy. He had led a hard life with willingness and resolution but he is very bruised in his mind about what has happened." Before he could say more, he heard a groan and they hurried to find Henge awake, staring up into the straw roof of his shack.

"Ah. You are awake then. Are you hungry for I have cooked something from your eel trap?" Orris said in as normal a voice as he could muster.

"I thought I ought to stay a while to help this lad who has obviously decided that you need looking after."

"I guess that's true." Henge croaked, trying to rise from his pallet. But somehow his limbs were not responding to his resolve.

"Stay there." Remonstrated Orris. "Here. Take this fish. I hope I haven't overcooked it?" Handing to Henge the skinned fish on a horseradish leaf. "Here Minos, some for you as well." He said, as if the situation was quite normal.

"In case you are wondering, I have decided to stay here a few days. Just to help get you on your feet. Tarsus has gone back to his encampment to get a few things you must need."

All this time, Henge was slowly eating the fish as if there was a lump in his throat, but he soon finished and was presented with some water. His food stocks were woefully meagre, but Orris did not comment on the loss of his stores of meal that had gone up in smoke.

Having eaten the fish, Henge lay back on his pallet exhausted. He wondered what was the matter but felt too tired to think and was soon asleep again.

For the moment, Lord Orris was not too concerned. He had known this kind of exhaustion after battle, and he knew that it would pass, if things around could be kept as normal as possible. It was as if a blanket of confusion and forgetfulness had taken hold of Henge and sleep, deep and untroubled had gripped him. So be it. Orris would be patient.

Twenty-four hours later, Henge awoke to another day and felt that the fog on his mind was lifted and he lay now, relaxed and flaccid, his breath coming in gentle waves.

He heard muted activity outside his shelter and for the first time in two days, wondered what time it was. The sun was shining in his face, so guessed it was early evening. Was it really only a day since the withy had been torched, he wondered idly. No agitated memory disturbing his mind.

Twenty-four hours later, Henge awoke from intermittent sleep clearheaded, free from wild dreams. All this time, he had hung onto the fact that Orris was still there and the boy Minos, who still guarded his sleep, was always at the foot of his pallet when he awoke.

Now he began to move his limbs and breathe more deeply. The iron grip that had taken hold of him, now seemed to have been released.

Just then, the flap that had been placed over the entrance to his bed, was drawn back and Minos appeared with a bowl of potage. The boy smiled his sweet smile of delight seeing that Henge had his eyes open.

"Oh Master, you are awake! I have brought you some food. I made it myself. It is good." The boy said happily. "And Lord Orris has been keeping the fish lines in action. We shall not go hungry." Henge turned to the bowl in front of him and realised that he was indeed ready for this appetising bowl of broth and it was soon consumed.

Delighted, Minos asked. "Do you want some more?"

Shaking his head in answer, Henge lay back on his bed, as the events of the fire crowded in on him. "Dear boy, that was good!"

"You will feel better now!" Minos asserted with a proprietorial air.

Henge gave him a feeble smile, quite devoid of the derangement previously evident. To tease the boy, he asked gravely. "And you have been looking after my mare as well, I hope?"

"Oh yes." The boy said earnestly.

"That was good. Now I must speak to Lord Orris, if he is still here? But I am thirsty, if you have some water nearby?"

"Of course. I will make you some dandelion and mint brew." The boy said solicitously.

At his reappearance, Orris was anxious to find out if Henge was awake.

"Yes, My Lord, and he is asking for you." Minos replied as he began to pour water into the fire-warmed pitcher crushing fresh leaves into it.

"Ah. You are awake, I see." Orris said with satisfaction.

"Yes, my Lord. How long have I been sleeping?"

"Long enough, I think. For you seem much better today." The relief plain to hear in his voice.

"I don't know how...what..." Henge' voice trailed away on the edge of tears.

Lord Orris put his hand on him. "Do not fret. There is plenty of time for these questions. But I will tell you that I intend to stay here for some while." He said reassuringly.

"You are in the middle of building a new house, I see. Much better than your last one. It looks as if you were in need of extra help to complete the basic structure. What was your intention? I am here to help hasten the plan forward if you want." Orris said to divert Henge' thoughts away from the past.

"Well. Yes, it is much bigger." Said Henge, slowly bringing his mind back to the task ahead. "I should explain that I had planned to have it ready before the bad weather comes, at least, at latest by the Spring. But..." He hesitated. A bleak note coming into his voice.

"Well. What is stopping you. You have the plan and you have the labour?" Orris reassured him.

Henge did not immediately reply. Finally, he said, as though the words were dragged from him. "Don't you see. My plans were formed...before...the fire."

"Well. Why are they different now?" Asked Orris gently.

The question was left hanging in the air, and Henge appeared to be far away. At last, he turned to Orris, who saw how distraught his face had become. He waited, giving Henge time to continue.

Then the young man spoke again. "You must know that I met someone at the fair who has promised to marry me. One of the Troupe of Entertainers. She will return from the West country at the time of the Autumn Equinox. I said they could use the headland for the winter.

"I had long known that my home on the headland was under threat. Indeed, that was why I deterred any curious eyes with my tales."

"No one minds my fishing activities but many might like to take my furnace over. Beako, for one, might have eyes on it, if he has ventured to explore, for he already understands about the use of firing a furnace."

"The troupe are young and agile, but soon will grow too old to be part of the entertainment. It was my plan that I would offer to train anyone who had an interest in learning my trade. More than one if they were so inclined. These entertainers are strangers from a far land and have met with much distrust. Well. I know how that feels and I aimed to give them a home at least. Added to this, I have met a maiden who is training my colt to use for the acrobatics."

"She is wonderfully agile and has such skill in tumbling. I saw her skill even on my untrained horse." He went on, the note of admiration there, in his voice. Then he was silent.

Orris waited to hear more, for he sensed Henge hesitate.

"Well, that is wonderful news and a very wise plan. What a gift you have for seeking opportunities." Orris said admiringly.

Minutes passed as Henge struggled to master his voice. Orris could see the dark clouds that gathered around this dear young man and he waited to hear what was troubling him.

"But, but don't you see, don't you understand. I cannot expect Lilia to come to live with me, if everything that I do, everything I planned, comes to nothing because of the evil intents of other men."

"If she stays behind with me in the Spring when the entertainers leave for the summer, I will be putting her in grave danger. If I cannot defend our home, what life would that be for her? For me to expect of her?" He said bleakly.

It seems that many men seek my downfall. You know of my history. After all, I was singled out for an acolyte in my first Tribe, by the priests. Then you know the story of my banishment from the Five Rivers Tribe for trying to protect my sister. Why do men seek to destroy me when I wish them no harm except to be left alone to make my own decisions in life without fear or favour. Wishing no harm on any man!".

The silence stretched away, for Orris knew that he had come upon the real reason for the young man's heartbreak. Then he said. "It seems to me that you are anticipating too much. It was a fine plan that you have been working towards. This has been a setback but perhaps there are others who do not like what these bullies might want to do and admire what you are trying to achieve. You are a fine young man and one who has the ability to drive forward with your plans and what you want for your life and there will always be lesser men who envy that spark of independence that you show."

"Remember, you will not be alone, for others admire your independence and fearlessness who have known this man, Beako, and have suffered such men before. They may be prepared to help you. We will speak more of this. But where you see only a bleak future with this young woman, and do not wish to harm her, perhaps you might also give her the choice."

"Have you no trust in her affections? After all, she is no stranger to the ways of bullying men. She has come from many miles away and has seen how people have treated them. Perhaps she sees in you, someone who would stand up to such treatment and provide her with a sanctuary. Have you no trust in her affection?" Orris gently chided him.

There was no response from Henge, so he went on. "Women seem very frail creatures but they are there for our delight and in so many ways, they lighten our burdens. Caring and sharing whatever life brings upon us. Do not underestimate her. You say that you have given her your colt to train? That was an act of great trust and I am sure she must believe in you also, to commit herself to a future here on the headland. My advice, is to build your house and give her the chance to decide. Do not underestimate her." He repeated.

Henge looked at Orris and hung on to his words. Then, into the silence, he whispered. "But I am afraid."

They looked at each other, the stark truth laid bare. "Dear Henge." Orris said, at last, very slowly, for it was clear that he felt the man's pain. "Don't you know that overcoming fear, IS WHAT IT TAKES TO BECOME A MAN!" He took the young man into his arms and hung on to him until he felt some stiffening of his backbone.

From the horse's stall, Minos had been listening and began to understand some of the complexities of life. But he had hitched his star to this young hero and resolved to take care of him. Henceforth Henge would be his liege lord!

CHAPTER TWELVE - THE RAISING OF THE BARN

Next morning, after they had eaten, Orris suggested that they first gather alder branches. They laid these flat on the ground near the proposed building. Measuring the required lengths they would need, they split the wood lengthwise and again laid them on the flattest piece of ground to dry out the sap and retain their shape. Next, they went to the river and cut the sedges below the waterline, as long as they could, before laying them out to dry on the bankside. When this had been done, they gathered them in bundles tied at both ends.

By this time, Orris judged that a rest was in order, for Henge had not recovered all his strength, but they were able to plan how they would raise the main oak beam.

With the added strength of the additional stallion and the mare, they planned how they could fix the main beam fore and aft by using the strength of the horses to cantilever the main beam into position. Twice the main beam rolled away but by securing it onto the cruciform end beams more firmly they managed to place the first end of the beam into position. They saw that the main beam was putting great pressure on the cross beams and they hastened to add buttresses to the four cross beams.

They laboured all day to get this first end of the beam positioned to be cradle by the cross beams. After all this, they knew that they would not be able to guarantee the stability of the first lift until the second end of the main beam was in place.

This led to the most difficult decision. To reverse the process and lay the main beam back on the ground. Frustrating, but they had achieved a great deal.

The day's labour had brought Henge alive again. He now saw how it could be done and he was planning another lift for the next day. But the most logical progress would be made by reinforcing the cruciform supports with extra cross bracing.

By now, all of them were exhausted but happy that they had solved their main problem.

In his anxiety and focus on raising his future house, Henge was forgetting his hope of a foal from his mare. All this straining and hauling was not good for her. He woke the next morning and remembered. What a selfish fool he was to risk his mare's pregnancy!

His elation of yesterday was brought to a crashing sense of reality. What was he doing here? Risking the mare for the sake of more manpower. Well, he must possess himself in patience or he risked losing the only thing that he could give Lord Orris to repay him for all his help. But for how long could he expect him to stay away from his own tribe?

It was as if the heavens were answering his question, for the morning had turned windy and dangerous for their renewed efforts and the lift had to be postponed.

Henge went to check his fish lines and wondered if he could fashion something out of metal to help them to secure the cross beams. What was clear to him was that more manpower was needed.

Meanwhile both Orris and Minos woke to the discomfort of a wet day with little protection from the wind and rain. Orris marvelled at how Henge had survived this windy inhospitable place for so long. Even the boy seemed immune to the harsh reality of their existence. He thought, rubbed his aching arms together to ease the stiffness of yesterday from his limbs.

Well, at least some food and warm drink would help to chase the weather away.

Outside the shack, Minos had begun to prepare a herbal brew, and was also stirring a pottage of sea cabbage and half roasted meal, into which were also some shrimps and molluscs gathered from the sea shore. He began to feel better already with the sight of this warming feast. This boy was certainly capable of many surprises.

From along the Larksfield could be heard the sound of horse's hooves.

Henge retracing his steps with his fish, hailed Chief Tarsus. "It is good to see you!"

Tarsus nodded in agreement, and dismounted "And I am glad to see you are recovered, it seems." He said, noting the return of purpose in the young man's stride. He turned to the back of his horse and pulled down two bundles wrapped in horse hide, from its rump.

Together, they carried these to the fire and greeted the others. "Good morning, I have brought you something to improve your encampment."

He unrolled the hides for their inspection, inside of which were several sacks of meal and assorted goods. He then spread out the two large animal skins for their inspection. "Do you think these will help to keep you dry the next time the weather turns foul?" Tarsus now asked, looking up at the, grey but dry sky.

Henge looked in wonder and gratitude at Tarsus. "Thank you indeed friend. We are sorely in need of what you have brought. Look Minos, here is payment indeed for all the good food that is cooking in your pot. Give Tarsus the first bowl of that hunger provoking brew, that will fill our bellies! Tonight, we might all sleep soundly, for these wonderful hides will keep out the bad weather." He said, with more of his usual manner.

CHAPTER THIRTEEN - A CHANGE OF LEADERSHIP BRINGS NEW WAYS

The attention to household chores and routine, hid the anxiety that Raisa and Mother Ava felt at the disappearance of Lord Orris. They were being closely watched by Lucca, now Leader of the tribe, who distrusted their protests that they were ignorant of her husband's whereabouts.

In truth, they were, for no news of any kind had reached them. His continued absence was a thorn in the side of this new leader who, it seemed, wished to show off his new status, to the fallen chief. With the man absent, this sense of superiority could not be reinforced and the only satisfaction Lucca could derive was to pester his womenfolk.

The other womenfolk and some of their menfolk, judged this as unfair. But they didn't wish to take sides against a new leader. After all, they had accepted him as their Chief and they weren't going to defend the fallen leader's womenfolk if Lord Orris was not prepared to defend them himself. All the same, Lucca's actions left them feeling uneasy.

This uneasiness had started, when rumours of his behaviour at the Roundwood Enclosure had become more general knowledge. Most of the Five Rivers Tribe who had been there themselves, had returned to their own Encampment before it was realised what Lucca had done.

When someone challenged him about the theft of the colt, he denied it hotly, saying that it was all lies to discredit him for ordering Henge's banishment, five years before. As, many of the Elders had sided with Lucca over that decision, they felt their only course of action was to side with him on trust. All the same, they were beginning to tire of his ways of governance.

The idea that every trip out of the village to visit neighbours, must be watched over by their new chief, seemed very restricting.

Most of them were glad that Lucca's high handedness was restricted to Lord Orris and his family, and did their best, to avoid any trouble falling on themselves.

Raisa and Mother Ava, suffered cruelly by his taunts. Two days went by and still no word from

Lord Orris, and the Lady Raisa was beginning to think that there was real trouble afoot.

* * * * *

Hengistbury.

The gift of two leather horse hides was most welcome. Together, the three men were able to construct a much sturdier shelter. "Well now, Tarsus, can you give us some good news?"

"I don't know whether it is good or bad. Beako is alive, but will not trouble you for a while."

"His eyes and cheek are badly affected but he appears to have survived the worst of it. Which means for the time being, he is harmless. But for how long? We shall see. I think you should have no trouble from that quarter, for a while anyway."

"It seems that all is well at home but your disappearance has been taken badly by your new leader! What a turnaround, My Lord! It seems that your Lucca is keeping a close eye on the Lady Raisa. Your own disappearance, without asking for approval first, has been marked and your family is being heavily monitored.

"How dare he!" Lord Orris exclaimed. "That is not our custom!"

"Perhaps not. Things sometimes change when someone new takes over. A gift of smoked fish might get through to them, perhaps?" Suggested Tarsus. "No message, except good wishes.

"No. No. That would immediately tell of our whereabouts!" Exclaimed Henge. "What a turnaround indeed!"

"Our prisoner who stole Henge's colt was duly chastised by the Elders of the Roundwood Tribe and chased out into the forest. It was their decision as to punishment. But he did not stay there in the forest, but hastened back to the Five Rivers Encampment before any witnesses to his shame had arrived home." Chief Tarsus continued.

Lord Orris then took up the tale. "I admit that I have been much taken up with a sickness that My

Lady suffered after our son was born and had allowed the hunters to see too much of Lucca in recent days. He had begun to plot against my leadership but I had thought that I had the backing of the majority of the council."

"I was wrong, for on my return, they had listened to his explanation and believed that he had been ill used by Henge' accusation of theft. There is a history of vengefulness of Henge by Lucca. I bear some responsibility for this. It goes back to when Henge was taken as a slave by the Five Rivers Tribe. I do not need to explain, except to say that Henge is a witness to black deeds and is a constant reminder of this, to Lucca."

"This happened under my command. I bear responsibility for Lucca's actions, but he is a vicious vengeful man, who gets more dangerous every year. As a young man, I thought his actions wild, but that day, his actions turned evil, and I should have stopped him."

"Now, most of the tribe are afraid of him and will not stand up to his posturing's. This sickens me. We are at present, a tribe that is very divided between the very old and the very young, for many of the children were swept away by the great hunger, eight years ago. Yes, now we have the young and foolish and the old and feeble with no solid middle. Only a group of vain and selfish hunters who wish only to aggrandise themselves and have no thought for the care of the Tribe." Orris explained.

"We took two slaves, to help with the hunt at that time. Henge was one and he was skilful and brave in the hunt. I was eager to promote him, for he shone with youthful talent. Quick to learn and easy to teach. I suppose I grieved for my sons, who had died that winter and my preference was a slight to Lucca who had headed the hunters and did not like a rival."

"Before long, Henge's prowess in the chase was rewarded and he was given freedom. He became a full member of the Five Rivers Tribe. This angered Lucca, and he plotted to get rid of Henge, by intriguing to banish him from the tribe for five years. For Lucca knew that Henge WAS THE ONLY WITNESS, to what had been done to the Stone Circle Tribe, that winter of the great hunger!" Lord Orris finished.

Same day: Five Rivers Encampment.

By now, Raisa and Mother Ava were very worried and kept to their task of gathering the equinox bounty from the hedgerows. "What can we do, Mother Ava? I fear that My Lord's absence is making Lucca very angry. Can we not leave here and go to my brother?"

"We cannot do this openly, for this would be just the excuse that Lucca needs to punish us as disloyal." Cautioned Mother Ava. "We must think of a way."

They were some distance from the centre of the settlement at this point and a young man approached them stealthily, appearing from around a tree, looking very afraid. "Are you the Lady Raisa?" He asked.

Raisa quickly looked to see whether anyone else had seen the boy approach and the two women moved to hide him from view. "Yes, boy. Have you a message for me?"

The boy nodded. "I was to tell you that "All is well'."

"Yes, yes, and….?

"Just that." He answered.

"But where have you come from? Why is My Lord not here himself?"

"I mustn't say anything else. I do not know." The boy said, frightened by the urgency of the question.

"But where have you come from? I must know this, at least?"

I come from the Riversmeet Tribe away to the setting sun, where the river below you, meets another river to flow to the big water."

"Yes, yes?" Urged Raisa. "Is that where there is a headland?"

The boy nodded. "I must go." And he fled into the trees.

The two women looked at each other, while the child, Horsa was collecting the fallen fruit nearby and was looking with great care, at all the maggots wiggling inside them.

"This messenger seemed very nervous. Why did he approach us here, away from the eyes of the hunters? And why was the message so brief. It is not like Lord Orris to be so. He would send me his greetings and reassure me of my brother's love! Why, oh why?" She whispered, by now much alarmed.

Mother Ava straightened up from her task and looked sombrely at Raisa. "Perhaps he is with your brother and did not wish this fact to be spread amongst the Five Rivers Tribe. Especially that Lucca should not hear of it."

The two women stood helplessly trying to make some sense out of such a brief message. "My Lady Raisa. Come, we will find some better blackberries on the top of the rise."

Mother Ava then said quietly to the boy. "Come, Horsa. I see some much bigger blackberries over there. Bring the basket. When we have gathered these, we will find a sunny place by the stream and have some food. Come. Come. Forget the maggots and beetles." Mother Ava called him.

"My Lady Raisa, come, we shall find some better blackberries, there. Look how good they are."

Raisa looked at her oddly, then realised that a decision had been made. She took up her basket and without haste, joined the older woman who was working the hedgerow with her basket over her arm, gradually working to the top of the rise. Slowly, Raisa followed her, all the while talking to the boy to keep his interest on what they were doing.

"Mother Ava. Am I reading you right? Are we leaving the encampment?" Whispered Raisa.

"Well. There is no time like the present. We are almost at the top of the slope where the woods begin. I think this is a perfect chance to avoid pursuit. The woods will soon hide us from view, if anyone if interested. So, we should be well on our way by noon.

"But Mother Ava, can you walk to the Riversmeet Tribe Encampment? It must be three hours walk, at least. And with a small child?"

"Well, we shall just have to carry him, if necessary." She said with calm resolve. You forget that my life has always been to travel with the tribe and I can do it again. If my back troubles me, I shall break a stick from the timber in the woods hereabouts which will help me."

"If the child tires we must make him a sling between us that he can sit in. Be of firm resolve, my dear. I think the time has come to follow the sun's path to the big water. The boy said he was from the Riversmeet Tribe on the hill so we shall head in that direction. If we take it steadily, we should be there by nightfall."

But they had forgotten about the hunting dogs!

* * * * *

Same day: Hengistbury Head.

That morning, the three men and the boy began their task on the new building. They cantilevered the central beam over the crossed end beams and secured it in place. Then they began the more difficult task of raising the second end of the beam onto the other crossed beams. The three men stood at this point ready with a pile of other short beams. As the horses began to pull on ropes attached to the same end, the three men lifted the main beam sufficiently to insert a short beam underneath it. By a series of short elevations and insertions, they managed to bring the main beam to the height of the cross beams.

They rested and shortened the ropes attached to the horses. Once again, they urged them on, and the main beam was finally lifted over the second cross beam, and braced by a second set of buttresses at the base of the cross beams.

By organisation, determination and brute force, of animals and men, they had succeeded in creating the beginnings of Henge' dwelling, and the fulfilment of his dream!

At last, it was accomplished.

Lord Orris looked at Henge when at last it was done and admired all the energy and inventiveness of the younger man. But most of all, he rejoiced at the transformation of the spirit.

No longer the desperate soul of yesterday, but a man with a future, who, again by his own efforts and goodwill of friends, had begun his headland home.

That night, it was a clear and moonlit night and the band of cheerful men went down to the big water to wash away the sweat of the day and swam and played, like children. All the carefree games of their youth were visited that night. They wrestled and dunked each other. They skimmed stones across the water and ran races along the sand.

Yes, all the memories of childhood that Minos and Henge were able to know again, games that had been cut short for them by an early end to childhood.

The two women walked steadily through the woods, urging the boy Horsa forward, with various tricks to excite his curiosity. Birds to name, or animals tracks to find. In this way they had perhaps, covered a quarter of their journey. As they travelled further into the woods, they lost sight of the sun and needed to mark the forest trail and the signs of their bearings. The lichen on the west side of the trees and bend of the branches to the prevailing wind. All these signs would keep them going, for they were surrounded by a complete forest and only by looking for them would they find their way out into the open correctly.

They had just rested for the middle of the day when, far away they heard the sound of dogs barking. The hunters had followed their trail! "Oh, Mother Ava, what can we do?" Raisa said in alarm.

"Well. If they catch us, we must say that we got lost in the forest. You understand? Lost. Not fleeing!"

Raisa nodded and picked up the child.

Mother Ava then said. "I know this wood and where there is a badgers' holt nearby. Quickly. We must reach that to throw the dogs off the scent. They ran further ahead until they saw a bank with holes all around.

"Quickly, cover yourselves with some of the soil. Rub it into your hands and feet. Cover the child with the badgers' smell. It is the only way to confuse the dogs!"

"Now, Horsa. Dear boy, we must play Hide and Seek, and when we find a thick bush, we will be very quiet. Some of the dogs will try to find us, but just remember we are going to find your daddy and we will not be able to, if the dogs find us. Can you do that?"

"Oh, Yes, yes." Horsa said, hiding his eyes. "Can you see me?"

Without answering him she rolled the child in the badger droppings and smeared them over herself.

Turning to the left, the two women fled towards a stream and walked into the water. Washing off as much as possible of the badger's muck, they continued in the same direction downstream until there was a large blackthorn bush on the other side of the stream. "Come quickly, Horsa. Here we have the perfect den to hide in." Raise went first with the child next, and Mother Ava last, carefully erasing their footprints with a stick.

"Isn't this exciting," Whispered Raisa.

"Are we badgers now?" The boy whispered.

"Yes, and we must be very quiet until the dogs have passed, for they are looking for the badgers." They lay there many minutes until the sound of the dogs had passed. Raisa looked down at the small boy and saw that he had fallen asleep. "Look Mother Ava, Horsa is sleeping. Shall we try to get more comfortable here and do the same. It will be better for us if we can rest for a while." Very glad to have these moments of respite.

While they rested, there came a trickle of raindrops through their shelter. Struggling to extract themselves from the bush, they were covered in scratches but were glad of the rain to wash away the last of the mud that had covered them.

Now there was no sun to follow but the stream flowed away so they followed it, hoping that it would lead them the way they wished to go.

They travelled more slowly now, uncertain of their direction. All they were sure about was that the stream would take them eventually to the big water.

Now, the sun was well advanced in the sky and the forest had dark shadows between the trunks of the trees. By now the band of travellers were walking at a very slow pace, carrying the child between them. The games they had played to hurry the child along had been abandoned as his steps faltered. Even Horsa was quiet now in his sling.

The sun could now be seen as a slight light ahead, but they dared not leave the course of the stream for it was there only true guide to the big river.

By this time, they were very hungry but ahead they saw a big bramble bush laden with large fruit, all ripe and juicy.

This was the first bush they had seen since they had been forced to abandon their baskets. Now they stopped to enjoy some of the berries and in doing so, saw that ahead of them, lay a valley which their stream was joining. A deep, dark river flowing south and there, slightly behind them to the left was exposed to view, the hill that they had been seeking.

Raisa sank down on a small hillock, overlooking the hill and valley beyond. "Look Mother Ava. Look."

Disorientated by the woods and hiding from the dogs, they had trusted to the stream that had entered the river at the other side of the Riversmeet Tribe's Encampment.

No big water could be seen, only a flat plain ahead and the rising hill to the side of them. But at last, they knew where to go. The river was flowing to the foot of the hill and then they had only to climb.

On the hillside, a youth had been chasing butterflies and had sat down out of breath, for these lovely creatures had outwitted him. Now he was surveying the deep dark river and the valley stretching out to the West.

From below him, he heard the excited chatter of a child and through the trees came two women and a small boy.

At first, he idly supposed that they were women from the encampment, drawing water from the river. To his surprise, he saw that they were the women he had spoken to earlier, when he had been sent to the Five Rivers Tribe.

He rushed down the steep side of the hill to greet them. "Dear ladies. What a surprise! If I had known that you wished to come to my home, I would have escorted you." The youth said, with panache.

"Hello, young friend. Indeed, we are glad to meet a familiar face. Have you come to make us prisoners or are we welcome to your home?"

"Yes. Of course. I will let my brother know." He started up the steep-sided hill, then stopped.

"My apologies. Let me help you up the hill. You must be tired by now. We shall find a gentler way ahead. Then I shall alert my brother to your arrival. Come. Take my arm Good Mother." Speaking to Mother Ava who by now, was pitifully slow. By small degrees, they almost gained the brow of the hill.

"Come young man." He said, turning to Horsa. "I'll race you to the top."

The boy, who until now had been carried in his mother's arm sling, now responded to this young man and struggled to take up this challenge and went racing the last few paces to the top.

Raisa clapped her hand in delight and relief that they had arrived, her son, now fully recovered in the hands of this playmate.

They walked slowly into the encampment with all the people watching their progress.

Awaiting them, was a man of medium height, with many of the features of the younger man. Tall and lithe, with blue eyes and blond hair.

"Greeting brother, Halstatt. I have brought you some visitors. It seems that they were not satisfied with my message this morning and have come to see for themselves."

"Welcome, My Lady. I am a son of Chief Tarsus. You must be weary. Come here, to our hearth and I will fetch some refreshments to you. Some goats milk for the little one, perhaps?

"Thank you. We had hoped for a welcome and you are very kind. We also had hoped to have news of Lord Orris and my brother, Henge, perhaps?"

"Do not upset yourselves." The youth said, reassuringly. "All is well for the time being, and for now, you must eat and then rest, for our home is yours until we have more news of those you seek."

My father is expected hourly, and will be able to tell you more. I believe your brother is with Lord Orris, but perhaps he will return here this night."

CHAPTER SIXTEEN - THE BOIL IS LANCED

Hengistbury: The same night.

Henge, Orris and Minos bade farewell to Tarsus and made their way to the new shelter in happy mood. For the time being, all their troubles had receded.

They petted their horses and gave them special attention. Henge was particularly anxious about his mare, for she had been more than willing to haul. The addition of the other two horses had made their task much easier.

Now, with all their tasks for the day complete, they could sit around their newly fitted fire grate in more mellow mood.

Minos busied himself with cooking. A task for which he was more competent than Henge. Years without a mother to cook for his father, had made it a necessity to learn, and he took this task over, eagerly.

The two men sat idly reminiscing about Henge' time with the hunt.

A silence fell, then Lord Orris spoke of what had been troubling him.

"Henge, I do hope that your time with us had some happy memories. I know I failed you. Indeed, I should never have taken you prisoner. For that, I am deeply ashamed."

"My Lord. Why? You rescued us from a life of drudgery and penance."

"But it was quite wrong of me to steal from the Stones Circle Tribe. It was in my grieving at losing my wife and children that we came to raid your village. We were angry at the priests of the Stones who had taken tribute of grain and livestock and left us to starve, when our crops failed and our stores were empty. They did not advise us well!"

"But it didn't stop there! Did it?" Henge asked harshly.

"No. No..." Orris sat there, sunk in shame and remorse.

"But you did stop short at us. Why did you do that?" Henge persisted.

"At one stage in the raid, I had been knocked senseless. At some point I came around, rather muzzy headed but I saw what carnage was taking place. I should have stopped them. I bear responsibility for what happened. But by that time there was a blood lust on them all and were beyond recall."

"But you did stop them. You did make them stop!"

"No. No, I didn't. I should have, but by then they were beyond control. To my shame! I am not fit to be a leader."

Henge saw his remorse and was quick to say. "But you did stop them." He repeated. "You stopped that vengeful cur from killing us. Your two slaves, who if you had but known it, were saved from a life of poverty and cruelty, from the time of my father's death in the chase."

"You were our rescuer, who treated us with dignity and gave us the chance to be better than we had been dragged down to be. Why, even my mother was pressing me to become a servant of the priests and all that entailed. With the offering up of my manhood and denying me any future happiness."

"No. You must not forever feel guilty on my behalf. You gave me back a life, only half worth living until then."

"Dear boy." Lord Orris exclaimed, his face a picture of grief...No, thankfulness. "I didn't know..."

"What I," And Henge' voice rose in anger, Who I cannot forgive, is the person, persons who...who, - HAD - and – DESPATCHED - the women of the tribe, TREATED THEM LIKE ANIMALS - especially the one who did - that deed - and killed my helpless mother."

Henge left the sentence hanging between them. They stared at each other and Orris, with dawning awareness, saw that Henge knew who the perpetrator of that deed was.

"Dear Heavens! So that is why...? That is who...?

"Yes…I saw with my own eyes, but not, I thank the stars my sister's eyes, every coruscating detail of that - HORROR - perpetrated by your henchman Lucca. Now the leader of the Five Rivers Tribe!"

With that, all the putrefying hatred for the huntsmen that were there that day, was expelled, and they sat there in profound silence, each thinking his own thoughts.

But the dam had burst and what was left of the cleansing reservoir of respect would be for another day.

For now, first they must 'break bread together'.

CHAPTER SEVENTEEN - FRIENDS UNITED AGAINST AGGRESSION

Chief Tarsus rode home slowly into the encampment, hoping to arrive quietly. But it was not to be, for his elder son, Halstatt, was there to greet him.

"Father, you have come at last. Was all well on the headland?"

He did not answer immediately. Then, "That depends upon what you mean. Well? Yes."

"Back to normal? No. There is a burnt out withy and little shelter as yet. My two horse hides have helped temporarily."

"In good spirits? Now, yes. Lord Orris and I were much distressed to see how shocked Henge was. He had been trying to get over the moment of the attack, but his friend, Lord Orris, helped there."

"It appeared that Henge had plans afoot to build a home for a young woman but was shocked to think he might have brought her into such danger, and for a while, was quite crazed with grief."

Lord Orris was familiar with such an affect. "Henge was in a state of total collapse, but we put him to bed and watched over him until the worse effects of the shock had passed."

"By the next day, the worst was over and Lord Orris was able to turn the young man's mind to the building that Henge had planned. He had already collected most of the building materials ready to start. Two heads made it a possibility. Three of us have made it a reality for we have just managed to erect the main beam onto the two cross beams." Tarsus smiled with pleasure.

"Well, father, the crisis is not over yet for there is trouble of another kind. We now have two, no, three visitors. The Lady Raisa, Mother Ada and a small boy!" They have fled from their Encampment!"

Tarsus looked at him sharply. "Well, are we to refuse sanctuary for two helpless women and child for such a sneaky snake as we were privileged to meet at the Solstice?"

"No. I agree that we cannot turn them away, but we are being dragged into a quarrel which is not of our own making." Halstatt pointed out.

"That is true." Said Tarsus to his son. "But if that had been our quarrel, with our womenfolk, would we have sought help from a friend? Would we have wanted them to be turned away because we might be the weaker party?"

"This we must consider, for it will affect us all. I do know that giving in to lying bullies, is not the way to lead a tribe wisely.

"If a man is greedy for someone else's home or wife or goods, should he be allowed to take whatever he wants? In times of trouble, it is the leader's responsibility to act for the good of all the tribe. – and sometimes to defend a friend from a common enemy."

"Come, son. We shall talk more of this in the morning when we have had time to consider."

"For now, perhaps you would help me off my horse, for I am weary and wish to sleep before asking any more questions, or giving any answers.

It is enough to say, that you did the right thing to give this band of weary women, your protection this day."

* * * * *

The next morning, all those that are concerned in our story, rose in better spirits and all thought of weariness had receded.

Lord Orris and Henge had reached a level of frankness that showed the respect they felt for each other.

No more the dreadful sense of guilt and failure hung about Lord Orris. That terrible winter those many years ago had been left behind. Now they could build respect in their future relationship.

Henge began to see how different a life Lord Orris had led with the knowledge of these past deeds, and the pressure he had been put under by his Hunters. Discipline had broken down and had ended with Lucca gaining control of the Tribe.

He was welcome to it. Henge thought. For it had allowed him to think that his own idea of bringing Orris to his side, was no longer a fancy. Here was the perfect moment to seek a realignment of loyalties.

If he was to feel secure enough to build some industry with his players, then he needed protection. Orris was the perfect person to organise this.

He remembered Illyon, his ironmaster's words about changing times and his insistence on making and hiding his fine swords and daggers for possible bad times to come. Would they be ready to resist the band of bullies that surrounded them?

Then, he also saw that Lord Orris must return to his tribe for his absence would be much marked. If Lucca knew of his own weakness after the first attack, perhaps he would take advantage of this to settle their differences. There was hate on both sides, but Lucca would never let his feeling lie. He knew that Henge had witnessed his most depraved act and would seek to silence him in whatever way that was open to Lucca now that he might know where to find the only witness to his foul deeds those years ago in the winter of famine. That witness who might himself seek revenge sometime in the future. for the deeds of yesteryear. To take action against the man who despoiled and killed his mother

Now Henge wondered whether it would be fair to involve the hill tribe in his dispute? Would he be taking advantage of their friendship to drag the whole tribe into this quarrel. Chief Tarsus had been a true friend in his own need, but he had a family to consider. Two growing sons to protect. Both young enough to be eager for a fight, but untried in warfare. It had been enough for them to act as guardians of their hilltop home without taking up anything more seriously.

For the time being, the two men and the boy laboured to enclose the roof with timber beams and slats of split alder branches, on top of which they laid the dried reeds and pegs to hold them down. Minos was able to scamper deftly over this roof space to help to secure the sheaves of straw and anchor the pegs.

At last, they had an open barn, roofed and ready to keep them rainproof. Now, they could move from their makeshift hide shelters. Progress, and a cause for celebration. They had laboured so steadily that it had not occurred to Henge to wonder why Chief Tarsus had not yet appeared.

He had left them the night before in great spirits to return to the Riversmeet encampment but had not returned. He began to feel uneasy and resolved to retrieve some of the weapons that Illyon had so carefully hidden. Surely, there was nothing to fear? But his uncanny sense of danger drove Henge to be prepared this time.

He left Lord Orris and Minos to see to the horses and to bring anything from the makeshift tent to the barn. Here they could find real shelter. If they had made the thatch thick enough!

Then he went to the secret hiding place for his swords and daggers and carefully selected the ones he wanted. Three swords of varying weight and daggers of suitable length. He looked again for arrowheads and gathered them into a leather pouch.

CHAPTER EIGHTTEEN - THE OPENING OF PANDORA'S BOX

So, this was Lord Orris's wife. Chief Tarsus thought. A beauty, he could see, and so like her brother! Did she have his bravery and energy? Tarsus wondered? Well, she had risen swiftly from being a slave. What had caused two obviously high-born brother and sister to be made into slaves?

There was no story that had reached this part of the land to explain it. But it was clear that Henge had the mark of destiny. His energy and industry were evident, settling the land on the headland, with authority and resolve.

Five years of progress until that fire. The work of petty revenge, all because Henge had championed a defenceless boy! But this man had enough pluck to start again to build his dream home.

Well, that was as it should be. If there was to be peace to prosper and build a decent life, bullies and greedy men should be resisted. Each to his own patch of earth. There was more than enough for all.

Henge had proved that by creating an industry out of stones on a beach, that had turned into ploughs and tools and...he sighed at the thought...yes, perhaps weapons as well. Without something to defend their piece of earth, they were but flotsam tossed on the sea.

For all their talk of resistance, without a means of defence, they would not prosper. He had come from a long line of warriors, but he had found this piece of hillside, many years ago. All lonely and unproductive waiting for him to make a living out of charcoal burning. He had prospered by his own energy and brought up a fine family of men.

Yes, he could defend his hillside, no doubt, but for how long? His resources were limited and food was never completely certain. He depended on trading his charcoal in exchange for his requirements. There was also a thriving fair at the junction of the two rivers in the valley below.

But he knew only too well, that mean and vicious men flourished when circumstances prevailed. A grudge, a vanity, a lack of perceived entitlement or the advancement of another, all could be the trigger for conflict. Here, these few days had shown that even standing up to this kind of man, in defence of the defenceless, could bring down reprisals on the bravest of men.

Well. He thought. These brutes would not be calmed by a peace offering and a desire to be left alone, for them to conduct their grievance away from his own life and living. Next time, the bully might wish to push him around and who then would come to his aid?

He looked long into the beautiful soulful eyes of the woman opposite and made his decision.

Now, he smiled, and rose to greet her.

"I trust you are refreshed, My Lady?" He asked. "That was a long and lonely journey you made yesterday. I am sorry I was not here to make you welcome. I see that my sons have done so for me."

"You are assured of a refuge here, for I count your brother and husband as my friends. Tell me, what drove you to take this journey? My younger son tells me that you received your husband's message. Why should you be alarmed by his words?"

"Thank you, my kind sir. I am relieved to hear your words. My husband's absence had been causing me anxiety for many reasons."

"Firstly, his departure had been very sudden. Almost without a word of his proposed destination. We were left bewildered and, exposed to angry words and persistent questions by our new leader, Lucca. He was very angry that my husband had not asked his permission to leave the encampment."

"This has never been our tradition. Our people often journeyed to other encampments for exchange of goods and had never needed to explain these things in my husband's. time as leader..." She paused. Did this man know of the change of leadership? She wondered.

"Yes, I heard this news from your husband. Such a pity...and that man!" Chief Tarsus said, a note of disgust in his voice.

"I heard that you had met him." She responded. "Then you know that he is a very vengeful man, easily affronted. He has been making our lives very unpleasant, always asking me where my husband has gone and setting guards to watch us. We began to fear his uncertain temper."

"You were threatened?" Asked Tarsus.

"Not exactly. We were made to feel that our whole life in the tribe was being inspected. Each day that passed without my husband's return seemed to anger him more. He suspected that my Lord Orris had gone to visit my brother, and as such was considered an act of disloyalty, considering the bad blood between them over some horse."

"I know of it." Tarsus confirmed.

"Well, when your message came, we were more alarmed, for the greeting was so short. It was not like My Lord. His message told us nothing and alarmed us more. Our position was increasingly being that of hostages."

"When your messenger arrived, we had moved to a hill on the outskirts of our circle, to gather blackberries. Mother Ava saw that the moment to leave had come for at that point we were near to a wood to give us some cover."

"You were not stopped?" Chief Tarsus asked.

"No, but soon we were followed. We heard the hunting dogs and guessed that they were looking for us. We then acted quickly and confused the scent for the dogs to follow, and after hiding for a while, continued on our way. But by then we were lost and began to follow another stream which eventually took us to your dark river much upstream from your hill. Once we were overlooking the valley, we could see your high point." Raisa explained.

"That was a long way for an old woman and small boy." He commented.

"Yes. Even my young son is still asleep this morning, when he is used to eating by now!" She said lightly, bringing their conversation to a halt.

"Forgive me, My Lady. I am forgetting my obligation as your host. We will talk again when you are ready." And he went to the women of the tribe to instruct them to see to their guest's comfort.

* * * * *

Chief Tarsus thought it prudent to call his sons to a meeting to lay before them the activities of the last few days.

They were not completely aware of what had been happening on the headland, but knew it was sufficiently grave to be kept in ignorance of the facts. That there had been a fire and their father was helping Henge, was all they knew but there seemed to be something more afoot.

First Lord Orris of the Five Rivers Tribe was summoned. Then last night, his wife and child had come, apparently fleeing some unknown peril.

Now, it seemed, their father must make them aware of the risks they faced as a consequence of giving these women sanctuary.

"I must first ask you, my sons, what would you do if the leader of the Five Rivers Tribe came looking for the Lady Raisa? Would you surrender her to her tribal chief? Is it likely that she would be in danger if she returned to her home?"

Dugo looked sharply at his father.

"I have kept more details of my days on the headland from you, for Lord Orris and I thought that the danger was under control. Two days ago..." and he went on to outline Henge's problem. "It seemed that the man that had stolen his horse at the summer solstice, is now the leader of the Five Rivers Tribe and a vicious man, if I have any judgement in the matter."

"You will remember his theft of Henge' colt and this and his subsequent punishment at the Gathering, will not have been forgotten. He was humiliated."

"Do we hand these women over to his care?" Tarsus asked them.

"If we do, are we likely to face other demands from this leader sometime later?"

"If we get demands from Lucca and ignore them, are we prepared to defend these women, and ultimately our home and right to this hilltop?"

"More to the point, what are Henge and Lord Orris doing, Father?" Asked Dugo.

"Well. Trying to get his life back together, but it is now time to acquaint them of events here. "Lord Orris must be recalled to our hilltop, for they are his women." Said Tarsus.

"But are we to hand them all over to this new leader, if he comes?" Asked Halstatt.

"That is what we must decide. Do we stand by and let them be taken by their own chief? Or do we stand by them, for it seems they are threatened, and avoid any demands we might have later from this leader, if he thinks we are weak?"

"Of course, it is possible that Lord Orris will

(a) Go back with them willingly,

(b) Refuse, or

(c) Retreat to the headland to stand with Henge against Lucca."

"There is certainly every reason for Henge to resist him and Lord Orris has been his friend.

The question for us might be.

1. Do we stand by our friends?

2. Keep out of other men's quarrels?

3. Wait until this petty tyrant picks on us, sometime in the future. After all, without realising it, we became involved when he came with the colt, for we handed him over to justice of a kind?

Perhaps after all this, you should also consider whether you think he is a man to forget a grudge? "In the meantime, I think we should send a messenger to Lord Orris to inform him that his wife and family are with us."

"I will go, father. I took his message and can tell him of your situation. At the very least, Lord Orris needs to be here." Offered Dugo.

"Go, My son. Make haste for I suspect that we shall have an altogether less welcome visitor before long."

"Halstatt, I have need of you to give me your thoughts."

"Well, I fear that we are not prepared to resist these seasoned hunters. Dugo is a boy and the rest of us, ill- equipped to fight this aggressor."

"If we feigned ignorance of our guests, would it buy us time to prepare for any action. Should we stand our ground as before and try to turn them away on the steep sides of the hill."

"What do you think father?"

"I see you favour resistance. You are right to assess our defence ability first. We have never been seriously challenged before and our weapons are few." Said Chief Tarsus. "I never thought we would have need of our weapons of war again. Now we may be able to prepare some defences. Cut some stakes to impede their progress, perhaps."

"Our biggest danger is fire, for we could be trapped inside a circle of heat." Thinking aloud. Tarsus now pointe out

"Unless we encourage them to enter a ring of fire as we retreat." Suggested Halstatt.

It was beyond the highest point of the sun in the sky when Henge saw a figure approaching across Larksfield. Instinctively, he realised that something had happened of note.

He saw that the figure approaching was the younger son of Chief Tarsus and he hurried to alert the others. "We have a young visitor. Look!"

As he came nearer, Henge went towards him in greeting.

"Hello, Dugo. You have news of your father, I hope?"

Dugo nodded.

"I do. Also, news of further afield. Yesterday we had three visitors seeking sanctuary!"

"Oh yes. Who were they?"

"Well. I think I must address Lord Orris first. Sir. Yesterday I took your message to the Lady Raisa. It was very difficult to see her alone. However, I eventually managed to tell her of your well-being. I then returned quite easily to Riversmeet Hill. During my late day's watch on the hill, I spied three bedraggled, weary travellers, making their way to our camp."

"It seems that, far from reassuring your lady wife and mother Ava, the very brevity of your message seemed to have alarmed them further."

"Good heavens! Why must they do such a thing. Did they not know that I wished to keep my whereabouts unknown in the Five Rivers Tribe?" Orris exclaimed.

"I understand that, but I was not being harassed by your new leader, Lucca. I can only half imagine all that has been happening at their encampment. It seems that they were hostages, awaiting your return, for Lucca... I run on. This is not my story. Suffice to say, your absence has enraged Lucca and the consequence might be greater than you suppose." Dugo said.

"By the stars above! If they have laid a finger on my family!" Lord Orris began.

"Calm yourself, My Lord." Said Dugo hastily. "They are well, but very weary. I think your presence is needed for there seems, more trouble may be brewing."

Then, Henge spoke. "I think that it is my business too. It is I that Lucca really wants and was probably very suspicious that Lord Orris was with me. But my sister and family were restrained, you say?"

"I do not know the details but came here to warn you that my father seems to have misgivings about our future safety."

"I knew it! My presence, or activity or place on this earth, is a cause for Lucca's anger." Henge cried, passion in his voice, they had never heard before! "And my sister, she is unharmed. You say?"

"Yes, Henge, and glad to be gone from her home. With nothing but the clothes they stood up in. Both women. The only one with any spark was the little fellow who was being carried, but who sprang up the last few yards in a race to the top of the hill against me." Smiled Dugo, to reassure Henge who by now, was agonised of face.

"Why does that man always harry me, except that he knows that I am the key to his survival! If he had left me alone, I should have buried my grief and knowledge of his dark deeds. If his guilt troubles him to the point of hurting what family I have left, by heaven, I shall not rest until he is vanquished!"

Dugo stared at Henge. He had never seen him so angry. What was between Lucca and Henge? He really did not want to know, for it seemed that it was enough to drag them all into its vortex.

"Calm yourself, Henge. We are all here to support you. This is not just your quarrel any more. If he touches a hair on my dearest, my son, my family!" Lord Orris exclaimed.

"Yes, and also mine." Dugo agreed. "My father appears to think that Lucca might perhaps attack our encampment. We are woefully unprepared, I think."

"No. Not in the future! Illyon my ironmaster, showed me the secrets of his art. He knew that this day might come. He made me an ironmaster too and I have not been idle. But I am afraid and angered that you, who have been my only support in my own difficulties, should have to be put at risk. You do not seek any confrontation and it is my involvement with this man that causes your alarm."

"That is true of all of us, but when a mad dog is set loose, who knows who will be next to be torn to pieces?" Dugo asked wisely.

Henge turned away and from beside his new home, he picked up five swords and various other pieces, axes, and shields, and arrowheads in quantity, ready to be fixed to their flights.

The other two stood amazed at this evidence of preparations for war.

"Good heavens, Henge! You mean, you made all these?" Lord Orris asked, thunderstruck by the quantity of weapons.

"No, not all. As I said, my ironmaster knew that sooner or later they would be needed. Perhaps we are not yet ready for such a step. We are not practised is their use, although Lord Orris, and yes, perhaps your father, Dugo, know the art of using them, but others in the tribe are not."

"Well, for the moment we have only the presence of these weapons to give us heart. The arrowheads are our surest weapons, for we are practised in hunting. Close warfare requires very different skills."

Thus, heartened by the sight, they prepared to leave.

On Riversmeet Hill, Raisa, Mother Ava and Horsa were recovering their strength after their walk and were being cared for and welcomed by the women of the tribe. Raisa's anxiety for Lord Orris and her brother, was not lessened when she heard of problems on the headland, and she awaited their arrival. By midway after sun-up, it was thought unlikely that Lucca and his hunters would arrive, but a watch was kept on the highest part of the hill.

Still Lord Orris did not come.

It was the time of early dusk when horses were seen approaching from the big water.

Chief Tarsus and his son, Halstatt, rode out to meet him on the south side of their hill. It seemed right to speak to his visitor before he confronting his family.

At the last minute before departing, Henge had cooled down and thought it wiser to let others decide without his passions stirring them up.

Lord Orris had proved his friendship by coming to his aid before. This time, there was a more serious implication to events. He must hope that their own interests would carry the argument for helping him.

Whatever they decided, he must help them to be better prepared for any future trouble! He owed them that at least.

His own issue with Lucca would have to be addressed sometime, for this man would hound him until it was settled between them.

In the meantime, he had plenty of preparations to help him defend his own small piece of earth. Minos and Dugo were sent to collect the most suitable straight bulrushes to attach to his arrowheads.

* * * * *

"My Lord, My dear Lord. Thank the Stars! At last, you are come!" Cried the Lady Raisa as she fell into his arms.

"My Lady, My Lady. Are you well? What has happened to bring you here so ill-equipped. That you felt so frightened, that you must flee?"

"Oh. My Lord. Lucca has been so very angry at your disappearance. Every day he has more angrily asked us if you have sent word. If we knew where you had gone. Who you were with? Every day his questioning became more frightening. He seems quite deranged and spiteful when we said we knew nothing. Of course, we did not tell him where you were going. All the time, he suspected that you had gone to meet Henge."

"But did he hurt you, or punish you in any way?" Lord Orris asked urgently

"Well, not physically. No. But he set a watch on us to report on what we were doing. A very close watch. We began to realise that we were hostages and would be prevented from leaving. We certainly began to fear his moods and believed that sooner or later we would be misused."

"Why did you finally flee?"

"When the young man came to give us your message, we were on the far hilltop outside the village, gathering blackberries for winter storage. Dugo, had realised that we were being watched but managed to give us your message quickly and then disappeared into the forest. It was clear that he had waited to speak with us when he thought we were alone."

"Why did you think something was wrong when I carefully said very little?"

Raisa looked lovingly at Orris. "But my dear Lord. It was your very brevity of greeting that gave you away! I am used to being spoken to in a much more loving manner." Orris laughed abruptly.

"You are right and clever as a fox, my darling woman" And he hugged her to him. Unable to explain the dilemma they all now faced. He was just thankful that she, Mother Ava and Horsa were safe from the hands of that monster, for now.

Just then, Horsa shouted and ran to him. "Father, Father. You are here! We had a great adventure yesterday." And Orris gathered his son fiercely into his arms.

CHAPTER TWENTY - ON A WAR FOOTING

Night fell and Minos and Dugo were set the task to cut and shape the feathers into the bulrush stalks and to tie the arrowheads around the end of the shaft.

He took them to the Larksfield and they erected an effigy of straw to practise their arms. At first, they were way off the mark, for their experience had been with flint heads, which did not fly so well. Not so high or so far and it took them a while to adjust.

To make them more eager to score, Henge attached smoked fish to a position equal to where the heart might be and laid down a rule that there would be no food until they had speared it. This sharpened their aim and their appetite and added a small amount of reality to the practice.

When they had scored enough 'food', they gathered round the fire hearth and drank warm infusions of herbs and berries.

Later, Henge gave Dugo the chance to understand the movements in the parry and blow of swordplay: a desperately short lesson in self-defence. He wisely realised that these eager young men would have better results if they were put to more effective use in ambush, or distant attack. Such little preparation! He thought, and sighed.

By now, the moon was rising and Henge was shocked to remember how near to the harvest moon they were approaching. Were they really going to be under attack from Lucca and his hunters? Surely, they would respect Lord Orris and the Lady Raisa. But if not, then he would be left with no alternative but to seek Lucca out and put a stop to his enemy.

He now remembered that there was more to lose if he didn't settle this feud. If he could not guarantee the safety of the headland, then he would have to release Lilia from her promise. His whole body screamed at the thought of losing her, but without a minimal guarantee of safety, he would not see her in danger because of him.

He lay on his pallet that night long after Minos and Dugo were fast asleep, watching the passage of the moon over the very starry sky. He wondered, with great longing, whether Lilia was perhaps also looking at the moon in the same way. This thought now made bittersweet, by his resolve to renounce their engagement, if it meant that he would be asking her to share an uncertain future with him. As the moon was at last, hidden by clouds, he slept. In dreams at least, Henge held his beloved Lilia in his arms, as he galloped over the headland into sunlit clouds!

* * * * *

Next morning after gathering the catch of blue fish and seeing to the horses, Henge took Minos and Dugo back to the butts where they practised their arms. He set them to wrestle and spring and took them to run over the dunes and along the beach.

They were young enough to enjoy the rigours of exercise that they were being put to. Dugo was the elder of them but not by very much. He had, however, attained a much greater height than

Minos who was still, clearly a child but who was more than willing to keep up with the older boy who did not exert his full capability in the contests.

But they were beginning to work as a team which gave them more than twice the fighting force, for they could look out for one another.

* * * * *

Riversmeet Hill.

By lunchtime there was still no sign of Lucca and Chief Tarsus was beginning to hope that Lucca had decided to forget about the women for the time being. Perhaps they would deal with Lord Orris and his wife and family when they returned to the encampment.

Perhaps the Lady Raisa had exaggerated the situation and they could all forget about the alarm!

The feud that appeared to be between Henge and Lucca was of an altogether different kind and he sensed that here was a cause for reflection. But wisely Henge had not pushed this aspect of the situation as a cause for them all to be involved.

It was reassuring to know that with preparation, they now had sufficient arms to defend themselves. They just needed time to practise these marshal skills, and form a possible battle plan, if necessary.

* * * * *

Two days of storms hit the coastline and broke all Henge's fishlines.

Retreating to the caves on the cliff face, they spent time breaking stones in preparation for the re-firing of the furnace. Both boys were eager to see how the metal was extracted from these red rocks.

They kept guard on the headland in turns fearing that the new structure would collapse in the fierce wind. There only respite was the warmth of the caves for the furnace burned bright with the increased draught of air feeding the updraft, making the stones red hot. watching with fearful fascination, how the rocks wept until all that was left was an ugly pock-marked lump of black substance. Henge explained that it was the beginning of the thing that men sought. This 'iron' that could now be made into swords and knives. Then they saw its beauty as Henge worked the metal alternating the rocks into the fire, then into water, then onto the beating stone, before them. After many repetitions, they could see the sword being created in front of their eyes.

When Henge had finished, there were wrought, two new swords. Lighter than the ones he had shown them in his store. These were specially crafted to fit their individual hands, so light that their movements of the blade were rapid and dazzling. No mighty sword to slash and swipe: Brute force and destruction. No. These blades were meant to be used with light thrust and away, using fleetness of foot to dance around an opponent, until a quick thrust could hit home. Legs, arms, throat, all aimed at, and away before a crushing blow was struck by their opponents' heavier blades.

They were shown how to make their agility count for more than brute strength. For they would stand no chance if they allowed themselves to be cornered. No, the open spaces were to their advantage. But they must not let themselves be caught in the open if horses were being used by their opponents for then they could be cut to pieces. The heavier sword then being used to swipe and slash the man on foot.

Henge had marked out his defensive line and they set to dig a trench in front of the barn. They lay a light criss-cross of twigs over which they replaced the turf to disguise the trench.

This, Henge explained to the boys, was to trip the horse and unseat the rider. "Nothing less could save them." He said starkly.

On the third day. they awoke to sunshine. "Today they will come" Henge thought sombrely.

As dawn crept over the horizon, he had sent the two youths to watch from the top of the headland and then rode to the ferryman.

"Good friend. Greetings." He hailed him. "I have few fish for you this morning as the storm broke my fishlines."

"Aye, I wasn't very busy either. No one wanted to cross in the weather we have had." Said the ferryman who shook his head sadly.

"No. But you will be busy today, I think." Henge said encouragingly.

"I hope so." The ferryman brightened.

"Well. I will bring you more to sell later. Now, I have a request for you. I am expecting a party of hunters on horseback, who perhaps will use your ferry. The tide is not favourable for people to use the ford crossing today and they may be in a hurry. If you are asked to ferry these men over, up to six, maybe, perhaps you could delay their passage a while. Take them across in twos, or threes. You know, take them in a number of trips, rather than one. The river will be swollen with rain, and make the journey more perilous. You know, the sort of tricks you can employ to make a little more money.

They will be heavily armed and their horses will all be dressed for battle. So, they will be heavier than normal and will weigh down the raft."

"Oh no. Henge! Why do they seek you?" The old man asked, much distressed. He anticipated his trade in fish disappearing and he liked this young man, anyway.

"Oh, it is a long story. Suffice to say that I am an ant that pricks uncomfortably in the sides of the powerful. They seek to squash this diligent insect, but forget that where there is one, there may be many." Henge said sadly and with that he turned his mare about, and galloped back to the headland

* * * * *

Meanwhile, Chief Tarsus had spent an uncomfortable time on watch duty in the wind and storm that raged around them. They knew that clever men used this weather to cover their actions, for the inclement weather left some enemies off guard. But their watch showed no activity at all.

In more benign weather they had a clear view of the whole watercourses below them. In those conditions, nothing moved without their eyes seeing everything that passed. But yesterday, there had been wild flaying trees and torrential rain to blanket out visibility.

They stomped their feet and flailed their arms to restore their limbs to action, for the rain had soaked them to the skin.

Returning to the fireside, they warmed themselves and saw that everything was normal.

The Lady Raisa greeted both men with a smile. "Come, warm yourselves." She commanded and for once they were glad to be in the hands of strong women. "No sign of visitors, then?" She asked lightly.

"I don't think so. Perhaps they have decided we are not worth it." Lord Orris said, unconvincingly.

"Where are my sons, this morning?" Asked Chief Tarsus.

"Well, Halstatt is on the big water side of the hill, trying to see the headland now the sky is almost clear again. But Dugo does not appear to have returned from his trip to speak to Henge."

The two men looked at each other and immediately a message of enlightenment flashed across their eyes. "Of course! What are we thinking?" Tarsus cried. They were not the prize that Lucca was seeking. Only a means to an end; to find Henge.

"My son has not returned, you say?" Tarsus repeated, dazed by the enormity of his thoughts.

"Are you thinking, the same as me, Lord Orris?"

"Why was Henge reluctant to come with us here?" Asked Orris?

"Because he knew what Lucca really wanted, and Henge plans to draw him to open ground. Not a wood covered hilltop full of women and children. He is the prize that Lucca seeks." Said Tarsus.

"But this is madness, for he is now only protected by children!" Orris cried.

"No. Not children, young men, who by now will know some of Henge's plans and who will protect him to the death." Tarsus said sombrely.

"You mean to join him" Asked Lady Raisa quietly.

They nodded and picked up their swords.

"Then I am coming with you." She said calmly, taking off her cloak. She tied her kirtle above her knees and asked. "Do you have a bow, and arrows, for me?" Looking Orris in the eyes. Suddenly he saw the woman in front of him, transformed into the boy, he had also once loved foolishly all those summers ago, when they had practised with the bow. Then he had known her aim to be strong and true.

There was something else in her eyes. An ugly look of introspection. She no longer saw the husband she loved but was looking far off in her mind. To his horror, he realised that she also had remembered the excitement of battle and of blood, and the strong pungency of entrails from her mother's body!

May the heavens protect her again! He thought. For he knew that she would come with or without him. This was the moment, just as it was for Henge, and she would stand side by side with her brother to avenge their own tribe.

CHAPTER TWENTY-TWO - LARKSFIELD

Hengistbury Head: Late morning.

Henge has stripped to his loincloth and cut his hair to the scalp to avoid any distraction. On his upper arm he has put torcs across his muscles and at his neck the same, below which was hung a disc, fashioned like the sun with a flash of a lightning symbol, lying across his heart.

He had sent the two youths, Minos and Dugo to the top of the headland to keep watch. They had a clear view of all the land below them and the harbour and hillside beyond. He had made his stand in front of his new building. An indication perhaps of his determination to hold fast to what he had achieved on this lonely ground. No use to anyone who was not prepared to defend it. A hundred times as many fish could be caught along the coast. But this was where HE chose. His ironworks were all of his own making and skill and took nothing away from any other man.

All he asked, was to be left in peace and that was only going to be granted him by an act of violence he abhorred.

Now, he drove the last man-sized stakes into the ground in front of him. Both as a defence and as weapons, if one by one, he needed to throw them.

Fleetingly he remembered the wild boar that he had killed on the Chase, and how close he had needed to be to aim true. He had smelt the breath from the wild animal, and brushed the long tusks in his final thrust. That second of heart-pumping suspension of time.

Then he saw them. Five mounted horsemen breaking cover from the bulrushes that lined the path to the ferry.

Two men, flanking each side of Lucca. 5 to 1. He wasn't about to make any mistakes, was he? 5 to 1. Not good odds, but Henge hoped the two youths that he had drilled, would stick to his instructions. He did not want to lose them both before battle had even started.

He knew that once Lucca had his attention fully engaged, that the archers could lessen the odds in one flight of arrows. And the horses, would the boys falter at the sight of these fine beasts?

They were ready to fight the men but would they hesitate at harming the horses?

He, for one was not about to let Lucca get away while he still had breath in his body.

The sun was almost at its highest as the sound of hooves pounded towards him. He could see the sun glinting on their armour but what could they see? Were they dazzled by the sudden view of the big water as it sparkled in the high point of the sun on waves? Ever closer they came, no thought of checking, as they pounded over the Larksfield towards the half-timbered frame.

Henge stood on a pile of wood behind the palisade of spiked spears. Clearly visible for Lucca to see. A clear temptation to men on horseback.

On they came, not checking their pace, arrogantly thinking that their way was unimpeded. But the storms of the last two days, had softened the ground and their headlong gallop was now impeded by nature, as the ground sank softly before them.

But they had their swords at the ready, and it was clear that they would give no quarter. No shout or check of the horses to speak to the man ahead of them. Henge gently eased the first stake out of the ground, then a second. 20, 25 strides away. Surely, they must break their horses' stride and turn.

Then, first the two left hand horses stumbled, sending the riders stunned upon the turf where Henge had dug a trench and covered it with soft wet clods of grass. Lucca turned his horse towards the sea in time to avoid the trench.

Then the other horses came on, as Henge felt their breath roll past him as he thrust first one, then another stake at the right-hand outriders. Two now on foot, and two mortally wounded on horses that attempted to jump over his stakes. But not quite, for the soft ground above the trench, had not given them the elevation required to clear the deadly impediment of spiked wood stakes and too late, the far outrider tried to turn his horse's head away towards the Fickle Lake.

They came down heavily, both horses and riders, right onto the spikes. Both man and horse now impaled and struggling in their death throes.

The other two now unseated riders, regained their horses and followed Lucca, galloping towards the big water. Struck by the sudden change in fortune, Lucca had veered away to the right just in time to avoid the deadly spears or soft trench trap. Now, all was confusion. Two of them on lame horses, two of them dead with their own mounts squealing in terror and pain. Those that were left, regrouped and circled towards the sand dunes.

Excellent cover for the two boys that lay hidden there with their bows and arrows. Before the aggressors knew what was happening, a hail of arrows rose into the air silently, and felled the first hunter. Too late to avoid this sudden hidden attack.

Lucca, now with only one of his four outriders still with him, veered to the right again and circled widely on the greensward, while his outrider took a tighter circle away from the dunes.

As Lucca turned to engage Henge once more, this time with less bravura, and more caution, he saw out of the corner of his left eye, three more horses on his flank.

Without stopping to engage them, he thundered back to where Henge still stood, Lord of all in sight. 50 paces away from the deadly spikes, he circled and spoke softly to Henge. Meanwhile his outrider kept watch.

"Henge, My friend! At last, we come to it, don't we!" Lucca cried menacingly. "You have been too long on this earth. I think I shall have to dispatch you like your mother!"

"Come out here, and settle this like a man." Lucca taunted.

"Why should I, Lucca. I have had no mercy from you, so far? Five to one against. Very chivalrous of you, I think. And what will happen when you have me, face to face. Will you instruct your willing cur to stab me in the back?"

"No. No. We'll settle this, like men." Lucca assured him.

"Now Troja. You know what to do. Let Henge and I fight like men. He is but a midget. We are lions."

All this time, Chief Tarsus and Lord Orris, had been making their way slowly to the spot that Henge had chosen for the end game. They would see to fair play.

The second man then dismounted and called. One, two, three, and the combatants began to face each other with caution. Once again, Henge remembered the sun and kept his back to the hill.

Then Lucca came on in a rush, with sword ready to strike, but Henge parried the blow. Again, they retreated and once again Lucca raised his sword to strike and Henge lunged forward but did not strike home. He twisted away from trouble.

Three times they each attacked. The older man was clearly more skilful but the younger man more agile. Only glancing blows had yet been struck. With the next engagement, Lucca attacked with fearsome speed and aggression, so that Henge was forced to give ground and his heel tripped on a clod of soft horse-thrown earth, sending him sprawling on the grass. The next second Lucca advanced and raised his sword for the final blow.

But it did not come. On the side of the field of action, Raisa had taken her bow and aimed her arrow at Lucca. The flight had struck him through an artery in his neck which gushed red blood over the ground, before falling at Henge's feet. "That is for the mercy you showed my mother." She cried.

Henge looked up to where the arrow had come from. He saw that it was his sister who had struck the blow. He bowed his head, not in triumph but in great sorrow, as he understood now, that she had known all along what had happened to their mother, that day so many years ago!

The hunter who had watched his leader Lucca, in the final dual, turned on his heels and galloped away from the force of such anger. Chief Tarsus and Lord Orris, took stock of the scene, unable, quite to believe what they had seen. Until Lord Orris took his wife into his arms, who was clearly in a state of shock.

Across the grass, the two youths ran towards Henge where he sat on the ground, unable to believe that it was all over.

Their excited chatter was stilled when they saw his face. A young man of 21, with eyes of great sorrow, who now looked as if he had seen the ghost of his past and was beyond rejoicing.

THE END

Over the bay on the clifftops that swept away to those ancient hills, inhabited by Dragons and Sea Monsters, could be heard a faint piping tune together with a roll of drumbeats. Faint at first, but soon could be identified as coming from a cavalcade of caravans and drummers, jugglers, tumblers and horses.

Slowly at first, for their music was more identifiable than their persons. But the bright colours that fluttered in the sunshine, was as good as any words to tell them that the Entertainers had arrived.

Soon they would reach the Larksfield and Henge might believe that his heart's desire would be fulfilled.

They had managed to make the ground free of any sign of conflict, and the barn stood ready, with walls and had been storm-proofed. The walls had been filled in with extra bracing and a mixture of clay and clunch-stones from the beach.

Round the fire hearth, more stones were placed, large enough to act as griddle stones and by their side were other stones to place other hot cooking pots.

Over all this Henge had devised an iron support placed centrally over the fire and on the top, hung a cooking pot, all devised from his own furnace.

Slowly they came, but their drums and pipes marked their progress around the bay, clear and uplifting.

Henge now stood with Minos at his side, and his eager eyes spied, at the head of the procession, a black horse and riding this tranquil animal was Lilia, his own true love, who had returned to take her place at his side.

He must make her aware of the life here on the headland. There must be no illusions, that this home would be grand, but he vowed to keep her safe and bring an end to the wanderings that had been forced upon them in their journey from a land so far away.

If she was ready to leave these travels that had been forced on them by so many distrustful strangers, then he would be her guardian, protector and loving lord and no one would ever uproot them again.

GLOSSARY

WITHY

A small shelter made of branches of trees and reinforced with bracken and mud and dung, hardened by heat from a fire and weather.

VIOLATED

Touched, ruined, damaged, entered by strangers.

DEVICE

Plan of action. Method or article to make something happen.

SACKED

Laid waste to, a town, or village by burning and stealing and killing all the inhabitants. Total destruction.

SLIVER

Long thin slice.

PLAGUE

Very infectious disease which kills large numbers of people. general term – not any particular kind of illness.

TRIBUTE	Church or government tax.
MEAGRE	Poor, simple, barely enough.
ANIMATION	Liveliness, enthusiasm.
INERTIA	Lack of motivation, lack of response to stimuli
TABOR	A drum which is carried over the shoulder when walking or marching.
THE EVIL EYE	A kind of black magic spell.
VAULTED	Jump over something or someone in a series of jumps.
CADENCES	Rhythms, flow of emphasis of speech. Musical sound which rises and falls in sound.
TO CHIDE	To scold, tell someone off in a mild way. Children
NURTURE	Care for. Look after. Keep alive e.g. child, patient. Old person. Plants, seeds.

DIVERGED   Gone on separate paths, ways
                    of living.

BLUFF   Small high point of cliff which
                    then falls away sharply.
                    Manner of speaking, generally
                    describing a man's speech.

EFFIGY   Representation of a God-like
                    figure. Sometimes a person
                    who is represented because of
                    special qualities.

GREEN MAN   A timeless representation of
fertility and re-birth. The origin of which is lost in
time, but still practised in deep rural communities,
together with a respect for the powers of the Yew
tree which contains poisonous fruit. Animals are
never put in a field that contains Yew. Old
churchyards will always contain Yew to ward off
evil from the graves of those departed

FETED   Made much of. As in admire a
                    celebrity.

SPAWN   Fish eggs. (noun).
                    To spawn. (verb).

IRRIDESCENT	Shiny and catching the light in different colours of the rainbow.
KIRK	Dagger, Knife.
SYNCHRONICITY	In perfect harmony. At the same time.
PALAVER	Fuss. Noise (Indian)
PREDATORS	Those creatures that feed off others. Carnivores.
QUALMS	Doubts, Uncertainties, guilt. Conscience.
TO PLEASURE	To make love to someone.
USURPER	Someone who takes over a position of power without the consent of those involved.
HORSE LINES	Where a group of animals are tethered. Particularly used where military horses are kept on campaign.

PIPE DREAM   (a) A hope that is unattainable or sincerely wish for.
(b) a dream experienced during a narcotic trance.

FECUND   Highly   fertile.   Able   to reproduce.

TO COVER   The act of a stallion mounting a mare. General animals.

TRAVERSE   Cover ground in a zig zag fashion, either on steep ground or when searching for something. E.g. clues.

COPPICE   Small stand of trees, light cover for trees that have previously been cut to ground level and the regrowth to be used in the making of fences, baskets. Etc.

ZENITH   Sun's highest point in the sky. Sometimes used of other situations indicating the high point. E.g. career, beauty, power, strength.

HOLT	The underground home of badgers.
TRANQUILITY	Peace, calm, unruffled by worrying thoughts.
BEHOLDEN	Ruled, owing obligation to anyone.
HUSBANDED	Cared for. E.g. Farms, Money.
CORRAL	Fenced in animals, e.g. horses.
AVARICE	Greed. Wish to own, envy.
COVETED	Wish to own something belonging to someone else.
DIVULGE	Tell about something secret, or private.
FIEFDOM	An allegiance freely entered into an obligation to serve and protect.

EMELIORATE	Soften. Oiled. Peace-making efforts.
PUSILLAMITY	Timid. Two faced, weak. Undecided, overruled by. Indecision.
ESCARPMENT	Sharply rising face of a plateau.
RUMP	Animal's backside.
REJUVENATED	Made young again.
FLAYLING	Whipping round in an arc.
VISCAROL	Gut wrenching. Deep down inside the gut.
TRANSPIRED	Happened.
AFFRAY	Battle, fight. Of fists, weapons or articles used to throw in a scuffle.
PRECIPITATED	Brought to action suddenly.

RAVAGE   To cause wilful destruction.

MISCREANT   Someone who breaks the law.

PROPRIETORIAL   Taking most authority over
                       goods or people or situations.

DERANGEMENT   Broken in mind, or more
                       severely, madness.

LIEGE   Follower of a leader to whom
                       the person has given an oath of
                       loyalty.

POSTURING   Strike a pose, attitude,
                       demanding attention.

CLUNCHSTONES   An East Anglian name for flint
                       stones.

HEFT   Physically move something
                       with great effort. Usually
                       requiring great effort of one or
                       more people, with the aid of
                       tools or animal power.

AUTHORS NOTES

This is a story of Iron Age Britain. Since, at this time there is no record of their written words, and how the people spoke I have had to imagine their names and ways of speech but where I have written of the land in which they live, certain facts are known.

They have left us great burial mounds with priceless artefacts which were buried with their owners, some of great sophistication. Rings of fortification are to be seen all over the South West of England and the burial of human ashes in pots (beakers) have been found in the area around which my story takes us. I have relied on these fragments of history to imagine the people and the way of life, so long ago.

Another clue I can give you is that the story starts on the great plain of southern Britain and follows the life of the people who lived along the many streams and rivers that flow into the Great Water at Hengistbury Head. For my purpose Henge's bury.

I have tried to keep to known facts from what we have learned, but of necessity can only skim over these with light brush strokes, for this is a book of fiction which seeks to paint a picture of how our ancestors may have lived during, what must have been, turbulent times and I have tried not to include anything that would have come at a later stage of our islands' history.

The exception to this, is that in telling the story, my vocabulary is inevitably 21st century in expression but not, I hope with modern vernacular or unknown facts.

New technologies bring great changes in their wake. The Iron Age brought people from far and wide to these islands to find these resources, especially tin, which travellers knew could be found at the far western end of these isles.

Travellers from all around the Mediterranean braved the Pillars of Hercules (Gibraltar?) to seek an island which contained this precious metal. This was most sought after, to make their weapons and helmets and shields, much stronger. Gold, Copper silver and iron all had waves of explorers who sought them out and these isles had them all.

Known and unknown civilizations used these minerals to change their lives in some way.

We simply see a small fraction of what was happening all over the world by the scientific confirmation of dates of artefacts that have come to light.

In reading this story of an ancient people of these isles, I would like to think that you might recognise a similarity of problems encountered by the people of these islands in every era.

Each man has his own journey through life to follow, but we are all seeking the same thing: to survive in our surroundings and find love and friendship to help us make sense of it all.

AUTHOR'S REFLECTIONS

The unprecedented times that we have been living through during the past two years has had only one benefit for me, to be able to immerse myself in the lives of this Iron Age settlement of Hengistbury Head.

So, I hope you will want to come with me along the road, to see what further adventures happen to my young hero.

It certainly has been an enjoyable personal journey with my characters during this difficult period of 'lock down' in our own lives.

NOVEMBER 2023

ACKNOWLEDGEMENTS

To my daughter and friends for their positive encouragement while I've been writing this series.

My special thanks go to Mick for his valuable insights of Ancient Britain.

HENGISTBURY HEAD SERIES

BOOK 1   The Storyteller of Hengistbury Head.

BOOK 2   The Iron Man of Hengistbury Head.

BOOK 3   The Orphan of Hengistbury Head.

This is the third of the Hengistbury Head series which completes the story of Henge' battle with the Hunter Lucca, of the Five Rivers Tribe.

Look out for future stories in the series and read more about the adventures of Henge and whether he makes the headland secure for the future of his bride to be.

Mel Flavell originally from the Midlands moved to the south coast with her family.

Her love of walking the Wessex highways and byways confronted her with evidence of ancient Britain. She was intrigued by the stone monuments and barrows left by our ancient ancestors, two of which were on her doorstep, stirring her imagination to write their stories.

Now she shares her musings with you in her tales of a young man's survival in the Iron Age.